USA TODAY BESTSELLING AUTHOR
Dale Mayer

HEROES FOR HIRE

GALEN'S GEMMA: HEROES FOR HIRE, BOOK 22
Dale Mayer
Valley Publishing Ltd.

ISBN-13: 978-1-773363-55-4
Print Edition

Books in This Series:

Levi's Legend: Heroes for Hire, Book 1

Stone's Surrender: Heroes for Hire, Book 2

Merk's Mistake: Heroes for Hire, Book 3

Rhodes's Reward: Heroes for Hire, Book 4

Flynn's Firecracker: Heroes for Hire, Book 5

Logan's Light: Heroes for Hire, Book 6

Harrison's Heart: Heroes for Hire, Book 7

Saul's Sweetheart: Heroes for Hire, Book 8

Dakota's Delight: Heroes for Hire, Book 9

Michael's Mercy (Part of Sleeper SEAL Series)

Tyson's Treasure: Heroes for Hire, Book 10

Jace's Jewel: Heroes for Hire, Book 11

Rory's Rose: Heroes for Hire, Book 12

Brandon's Bliss: Heroes for Hire, Book 13

Liam's Lily: Heroes for Hire, Book 14

North's Nikki: Heroes for Hire, Book 15

Anders's Angel: Heroes for Hire, Book 16

Reyes's Raina: Heroes for Hire, Book 17

Dezi's Diamond: Heroes for Hire, Book 18

Vince's Vixen: Heroes for Hire, Book 19

Ice's Icing: Heroes for Hire, Book 20

Johan's Joy: Heroes for Hire, Book 21

Galen's Gemma: Heroes for Hire, Book 22

Zack's Zest: Heroes for Hire, Book 23

Bonaparte's Belle: Heroes for Hire, Book 24

Noah's Nemesis: Heroes for Hire, Book 25

Heroes for Hire, Books 1–3

Heroes for Hire, Books 4–6

Heroes for Hire, Books 7–9

Heroes for Hire, Books 10–12

Heroes for Hire, Books 13–15

About This Book

Galen had plans to kick back and relax, but Levi needs someone to help out Zack, a friend of his. When Levi asks Galen, he's game. There's a little too much sugary sweet true love going on at the compound for him and his single state to handle. Then he meets Gemma and her sister, the real reason Zack was looking for help.

Gemma learned a long time ago how to handle her sister and her niece. When the two end up in deep trouble, Gemma drops everything and takes charge. But it's dangerous, and she needs help. Galen wasn't what she had in mind, but her heart is open and willing. Her body? Well, it's good to go when a meet-and-greet leads to love at first sight.

Only the situation is dangerous, and she has to stay focused—until the truth comes out, and she finds out what's really at stake.

Sign up to be notified of all Dale's releases here!
https://smarturl.it/DaleNews

Prologue

WHEN GALEN ALRICK walked into the kitchen of Ice and Levi's compound, he felt pretty decent. As Harrison looked up at him with a grumble, Galen's eyebrows shot up. "Well, *I* thought it was a good day," he said with a laugh.

"While you guys solved your problem," Harrison said, "we got the brakes put on ours."

"Yeah, you were supposed to give us a hand, weren't you?" Just enough gentle rivalry existed between the two groups—Bullard's crew versus Levi's crew—for Galen to rib Harrison a little bit over this one. Galen originally had worked for Bullard for a good seven years, but now Galen was in an exchange program here, and he wasn't exactly sure what his future held. He'd already talked to Bullard about it prior to leaving, wondering if it were time to move on and to do something else.

Bullard had shrugged and smiled. "You let me know if you want more work," he said. "You're always welcome here."

But the two teams had heard about Johan's decision to come work for Ice, and Galen had jumped on board with that, wondering if the change would be enough for him. But now he was here and had completed the first job—and damn fast too. Not at all the type of job he was used to, but it had been kind of fun. In fact, being here at Levi's compound was the same but different—and a great experience. He was glad he came.

"Did Johan come back with you?" Harrison asked.

Galen snorted. "No, he and Joy will stay and pack up her stuff." Johan had met Joy on the last case, and they had hit it off in a big way. Galen was happy for them. The job had been an instant lesson on how, no matter where you were in the world, the problems were the same: people would be people.

"Did Joy quit?" Harrison asked.

"She got a nice little paycheck to disappear," he said. "Kai would have stayed for a couple extra days to give them a hand, but everything in Joy's sublet apartment got trashed, so not much left to pack up. Joy had some banking and whatnot she wanted to do, plus some meetings to wrap up."

"And did Joy want to leave? She at least had a job there."

"Exactly. She had a job. It wasn't exactly a great job, but it was something that paid the rent. That's part of the reason why we were there a bit longer. We had to talk with the guy she had subleased the apartment from and the building manager. She and Johan are in Houston looking for a place for her now."

"You know that she could probably move in here at the compound in the meantime."

"I don't think she'd be too comfortable with that kind of arrangement," Galen said. He walked over, poured himself a cup of coffee, put it down beside Harrison, then walked back to the coffee server. "The thing about living here is that it's got some serious side benefits." He looked at the pan of fresh warm cinnamon buns, with the icing still melted all over the top.

"That's the second tray already," Harrison said good-naturedly. "I don't know how Bailey and Albert do it, but they just keep the food coming."

"And it's a divine system." Galen gently eased a cinnamon bun off the big tray, put it on his plate, and returned to the table, sitting down. "Working here isn't exactly what I thought it would be."

"That's because you had a simple job," Harrison said with a snort. "Some of the jobs are pretty ugly."

"I can do ugly," Galen said comfortably.

"I'm glad to hear that," a woman said, her sharp voice coming from the other side of the room.

Galen looked up to see Ice walking toward him with a clipboard. He grinned. "Do you ever run out of work for us?"

"No." She sat down somewhat awkwardly, given the slight belly she now sported. The fact that she was pregnant in the middle of all this chaos, yet she handled it all so well, was amazing. It also showed just how messed up the world was, given she was as busy as she was.

"Isn't it time for you to get an assistant?"

"I have at least two or three of them now, but it's never enough," she complained good-naturedly. "This will ground me for a few months, but it shouldn't be too bad after that."

"The payoff will be worth it," Galen said.

She beamed at him. "It certainly is in my case," she said. Tapping her clipboard, she looked at him. "So, you can do ugly, can you?"

"I can also help Harrison on this art job."

"Nope, we've been told to butt out of that one. The insurance company is bringing somebody in, and the cops don't want everybody crossing the line, so it's on hold."

"But the fresher it is—"

She shrugged. "I can't do anything about it. So, in the meantime, Harrison will work it on his own, quietly in the background, while you head off to Germany to meet up with Zack."

Harrison sucked in his breath and glared at Ice. She just smiled benignly at him. "Did you arrange this with my wife?" he asked.

"Nope," she answered, "but you wanted the art job, so you got the art job."

"You said it was on hold," he protested.

"But you also know it'll come back on our plate eventually, so no point in you being completely green when that happens. You might as well get up to speed now."

"It could be a big waste of time and money," he warned.

She smiled. "It could be, but we've rarely had any of those, so that's your job."

He nodded. "In that case, I'll get on it. I suspect a lot of it is cyberstuff anyway." He poured himself another cup of coffee and quickly disappeared.

Galen looked at her and smiled. "You get jobs of all kinds here, don't you?"

"I do," she said.

"So, who is Zack?"

"Somebody we've been looking at working with for a couple years," she said. "He's in Germany right now, waiting for you."

"Then I better get packing." He pulled off another piece of the cinnamon bun and sat here quite comfortably, in absolutely no rush.

"You fly out in two and a half hours," she said, "so you'll be tight for time anyway."

He nodded. "I'm already packed, so I'll sit here and enjoy this."

She nodded. "Take one with you, if you want."

"I might just do that," he said, then motioned at her clipboard. "You gonna give me any idea what I'm going into?"

She looked up at him, and her eyes twinkled.

His stomach fell. "Please don't let it be some ridiculous waste of time."

"How do you feel about beer?"

He brightened. "I love beer. But isn't it kind of cliché to send me to Germany to look after some beer issues?"

"Well, a lot of beer could go with the job," she said with a laugh. "Or at least afterward, if you need it."

"Now that I'm up for." He grinned. "But you're still not talking."

"One of the biggest breweries over there is having some issues with theft, but that's been compounded by the death of the new manager. But we aren't sure of all the details, and Zack said he needs backup. So you're it."

"If you say so." He popped the last piece of the cinnamon bun into his mouth, then picked up his cup and threw back the last of his coffee. "Am I driving to the airport and leaving the vehicle there or catching a ride?"

She shook her head. "Levi is taking you in. He's got a bunch of stuff to pick up in town anyway."

"Look at you guys," he said. "The owners of the company and you're both grounded."

She shrugged. "We're grounded all right but, this time, by choice." She patted her tummy.

Chapter 1

L ANDING IN BERLIN was one thing, but trying to do a transfer through the massive airport wasn't the easiest when his first flight came in forty minutes behind schedule. Galen made his next flight by mere minutes, earning a glare from the gate attendant. He gave her a winning smile. "Not my fault the flight was late."

She didn't answer, just checked his boarding pass, scanned it, and nodded toward the doors.

He took the long path to the plane with quick, easy strides, and the door of the aircraft was buckled up behind him as he walked down the aisle to find his seat. Sure enough, as was his luck, he was in between two little old ladies. He stared at the seat, then shook his head and tossed his bag up in the top, thankful there was a little bit of room. Often, when you were the last passenger, there wasn't even that.

He took a seat between the women, whom he discovered were friends, and, from the looks of things, they were settling in for a good chat on the flight. Groaning silently, he sank deeper into his seat. It sounded like it was time to meditate as the two old hens cackled back and forth, completely oblivious to the fact that one of them could have switched seats with him, putting them together instead of talking over him.

He closed his eyes, intent on tossing around the minor details he had on the case so far. He had a little bit of information on his phone that he'd read on the way over, but this flight was a short jump from Berlin to Munich, thank heavens. It seemed to be even shorter than he expected, as they were touching down before he'd even had a chance to adapt to the awkward seating arrangement.

When he finally got off the plane and headed outside, he looked around for his ride. The problem was, it wasn't like anyone held up a sign with his name on it. But Galen noted one guy, standing off to the side, a hard look on his face, as he leaned against one of the center posts, his arms crossed over his chest. The glare on his face said he hated being here. Galen understood. He walked over, stood in front of him, and reached out his hand. "Hello, Zack. I'm Galen."

Zack straightened slowly with surprise, then reached out and shook hands. "How did you know it was me?"

"Because you're the only other guy, besides me, who looks like you'd rather be anywhere else but here."

Zack laughed. "Yep," he said. "I prefer to travel by private jet, or give me a backpack and let me go through the woods, but a million people all crowded into one space trying to go in a million different directions? Hell no." Zack pointed the way to his ride.

Once in the vehicle, Galen looked at the small pickup truck. "Is this yours?"

"It is for this job," Zack said.

Galen nodded. He wasn't too sure about the lack of information—on this job and on his partner for this job—but figured that he'd get to know more about this op and Zack over time. Some guys ended up being the strong, silent type, never saying more than two words. "Do you have the details on the job? I know next to nothing."

"Yep," he said. "A guy was murdered."

"What?" Galen said. "Ice never mentioned anything about a murder. She said something about him dying but I didn't realize it was a murder."

"The local police didn't think it was connected to the goings-on at the brewery."

"And that's related to the brewery how?"

"Joe worked for the beer company. It's a massive production system. He was in management, looking to make some changes in the sales distribution, as well as implementing new security measures at the brewery, which made him very unpopular as well. Seems the first break-in was at the brewery, which followed two minor thefts. Then the second break-in was at Joe's home. But it was only made to look like a burglary," he said.

"Is that something worth murdering for?"

"Well, Joe was one of the few truly honest guys I've ever known," Zack said. "He took over from the guy before him who is facing two charges of embezzling company funds."

"Normally companies just fire them or lay them off," Galen said. "So it must have involved enough money that they couldn't afford to do that."

"Yes, but it only was by Joe's hand that his predecessor's been ID'd."

"So he made enemies long before his first day on his new job. And changes always make existing staff pissed off. No one is ever ready for those. And if he made a bunch of changes ..."

"Lots of them. And he made lots of enemies at the same time. Joe was not popular when seen as the guy who took down his boss and who then took his boss's job, especially when not knowing all the particulars. Although no one had anything nasty to say about him personally. Only that he was a hard-ass."

"So this sounds like more of a criminal case for the cops, right?" Galen asked cautiously. "Why are we involved?"

"Well, it was a job for the local cops," Zack said, "until I found out Joe's wife and kid are missing."

He studied Zack's profile for a long moment. "So that's when you made the call for backup."

"Yes. I didn't like doing it either." Zack turned and gave him a hard look. "You used to work for Bullard?"

"Technically I probably still do," he said with a laugh. "I went to the US to work for Levi for a bit to get a change of scenery."

"The scenery never changes." Zack had a world weariness that was hard to miss. "The shit's always the same. The trees might look different, but I can't even count on that."

Galen understood what he was saying. "So I don't understand what's happening with Joe's wife and kid."

"Joe and his wife had been having some problems, with some definite infighting going on," he said, "but nothing bad. When the kid didn't show up at school a couple days ago, however, the school called the house, and nobody answered. The cops were called at some point on the truancy element, and they said that she appears to have left town."

"And could she have?"

"Of course she could have. She's an adult with free will and all that," Zack said, "but she wouldn't have."

"And how do you know?"

"Because I know her."

Something in his tone of voice made Galen wince. "As in you *know her*, know her? Like, she is special to you? Or, as in, you knew her because she was Joe's wife?" He tried his damnedest to keep his tone neutral, but it was a little hard.

"I *know her*, know her," he said flatly. "But not that way. At least not now. We used to go out, years ago."

"Okay," Galen said, feeling a little bit better. "Do you have any idea where she would have gone?"

"No," he said. "Her house is untouched. Her purse, cell phone, and vehicle are all still there."

"Shit," Galen said. "That's not cool."

"YOU SURE WE'RE doing the right thing, Gemma?" Rebecca asked quietly. Her voice was a soft echo in the dark interior of the car. They'd been on the road for over an hour. And this wasn't the first time her younger sister had asked her the same question. Rebecca seemed to think Gemma was making a big deal out of nothing.

Nothing Gemma could say had changed her baby sister's mind. They were in danger. All three of them most likely. Gemma would do what she could to keep her eight-year-old niece and her own sister safe. And that meant doing what she was doing. "I'm sure we're doing the only thing we can right now," Gemma said quietly. They were both keeping their tones down because Rebecca's daughter was in the back seat.

"So you say, but we don't have any proof that we're in danger."

"The proof will happen when it's too late," Gemma said. "You know Joe was murdered."

"Maybe," she said. "We've sure gone to an elaborate scheme to get away from there. At least we should have told Zack."

"You may trust Zack, but remember? I don't know him

as well," Gemma said.

"That's because you've always been angry at the way we broke up."

Gemma just shrugged. She wouldn't go over old history right now. She had done what she thought was best here, and it was turning her life upside down too, but she was determined to keep Rebecca and Becky safe.

"I don't understand why you think they wouldn't find the cabin."

"They'll find Joe's cabin probably," she said, "and we'll leave a trail to say we were there but disappeared again."

"Why?"

That damn whine was back in her sister's voice. Gemma should be used to it. Whenever life didn't go Rebecca's way, she'd get that same irritating tone in her voice. "For whoever is now looking for Joe's family," she said harshly. "He was murdered, no doubt about that."

In a small voice, Rebecca said, "The police said it was a burglary gone bad."

"It wasn't a burglary gone bad, Rebecca," she snapped. "It was a murder made to look like a burglary gone bad."

Her sister sank back in the seat beside her. "I've lost my world," Rebecca muttered. "And you don't care."

At that, Gemma softened her voice. "Sweetie, I know. But it's more important to keep you and your daughter alive."

There was a long silence before Rebecca finally gave in and said, "I hope you know what you're doing."

"I don't," she said, "but I'm doing what I think is right."

"And I think what's right was staying at home, where the police could get in touch with me."

"Maybe," she said. "And then what? We have to take a

gamble on this and do what we need to do."

"But what if we're wrong?"

"Then we're wrong, and we'll face the consequences." She knew her sister didn't like hearing that at all, but it was what Gemma could do. She didn't know how else to help. She'd been traveling for work when she'd come home to this mess. She rented an apartment here, and rented out her New York apartment for the half year she'd been here. With her sister's move to Germany a few years ago with Joe's job, she spent as much time as she could over here in order to see her only two family members. She had been staying at her sister's house after Joe's death, when she'd realized that somebody was trying to get into the place. She'd scared them away once, around midnight, but they had come back soon afterward to try again. That's when she knew somebody was more than determined to get in. She called in the cops yet again. Gemma knew her sister and niece were in even bigger trouble.

And the more she investigated her sister's life, the more she realized that Joe's death was a murder and not a burglary.

After several hours the cops left. Then Gemma took the better part of the day to prepare for their trip. Instead of going back to her own house or even contacting the people who had rented it to her, Gemma had taken out a decent amount of cash from several ATMs, plus she still had leftover cash from her traveling funds. She'd asked to borrow a car from a friend who had several, and he'd given his permission, telling her to just let him know when she didn't need it anymore.

"Obviously you need this for some problem," he said, "so, if you need other help, let me know."

She smiled at him. "I have to go on the run for a bit."

With a nod, he said, "In that case, the envelope in the glove box will come in handy."

After she got into the vehicle, she had found little wads of cash stashed throughout. But then her friend had lots of it and lived on the edge himself. She drove back to her sister's place, actually happy to have night falling as she packed them up.

She'd parked down the road and made several quiet trips in the dark as she loaded up everything needed for them to leave. They had moved Becky into the back seat, still asleep and bundled up with blankets and pillows. Her sister didn't go so easily, arguing and complaining about the whole concept. Casually Gemma had made sure Rebecca left her purse, wallet, and cell phone in the house, then had given her a burner phone and another purse once they got on the road, canceling her cards as they drove.

"When will we stop?" Rebecca asked.

"I have to get gas up ahead," she said. She pulled into the gas station and turned to look behind her. Nothing but darkness. Dawn wouldn't arrive anytime soon. She'd been driving for hours already. It didn't feel like it was enough.

"I think we should call Zack," Rebecca said, still sounding surly.

"Maybe we will," she replied. "We'll talk about it when we get there."

"How much farther?"

"Another hour."

"Do you think he would come?"

"Probably," she said, "he's always been soft on you."

The awkward silence inspired her to turn and look at her sister. "And you're still soft on him." She spoke the words softly and shrugged.

Only Gemma knew that Becky could be Zack's. Or Joe's. Most likely Joe's. Rebecca had never confirmed that though, so ... that was their problem. The fact that Rebecca had walked away from Zack when she was pregnant, and that Zack had walked away at the same time, spoke volumes about their need to work out their communication issues. Maybe now they'd have a chance, but Gemma didn't want anything to do with it. She liked her life. She traveled a lot for her own business, as a contractor in medical software, and that suited her well.

Hopping out at the gas station, she quickly filled up the vehicle, then walked inside and paid cash, using a hat to keep her face away from the cameras. She didn't even take time to get coffee or anything.

Walking back out, she hopped into the vehicle to find Rebecca curled up in the corner, the burner phone beside her. She looked at it and then her sister. "You called him, didn't you?"

Shamefaced, Rebecca nodded. "He can help, you know?"

"Maybe," Gemma said, her tone harsh. "Or maybe he'll just bring whoever's after you right to us."

"He's not like that."

"No, but he's dangerous in his own line of work."

The burner phone buzzed. Rebecca snatched it up, but Gemma reached across and grabbed it from her hands. "What the hell do you want?"

"Ah, Gemma," Zack said.

But in his tone was obvious relief. She heard and noted it, but, at the same time, she glared at her sister. "If you'd wanted to help," she said, "you should have done it a while ago."

"I thought she'd be okay."

"Well, you were wrong," she snapped.

"Fine," he said. "Where are you taking her?"

"To a cabin."

"If it's Joe's cabin, you know they'll follow you there."

"Which is why we're going there," she said, "and then we'll bounce in a few hours, past that point."

"I want to know your itinerary."

Just then another voice came over the phone. "My name is Galen. Don't try to do this on your own."

"Just who the hell are you?" she snapped.

"Somebody Zack called in as backup, to help track Rebecca down."

She stopped at that. "Well, if he knew she was in danger, why the hell didn't he scoop her up and take her away in the first place? And obviously she doesn't need to be tracked down. All he had to do was call her."

"I already told you all you need to know." His tone was smooth. "Where are you?"

"Somewhere else. For all I know," she said, "you're part of the group who killed Joe."

"Well, I'm not," Galen said, "but I can see the possibility of you worrying about that. Although, if you know Zack, you know that's not possible."

"Says you," she said. She kept driving and thought about what to do.

"We'll meet you at the cabin," he said and hung up.

She tossed the phone down and stared at her sister in disgust.

Chapter 2

GEMMA PULLED INTO the cabin's driveway in the wee morning hours, checking the dashboard to see it was coming up on four o'clock. Her sister and niece were sound asleep. Gemma drove down the long gravel road up to and around the cabin to the rear of it. Parking, she let out a slow sigh.

Rebecca woke up. "Where are we?"

"At the cabin."

"I don't even know why you bother," Rebecca said. "I want to go in and sleep, but you won't let me do that before we leave again."

"You'll sleep for a few hours," she said, "but that's all." With that, she got out and walked up to the cabin, leaving the other two in the car. Unlocking the front door, she stepped in. This was Joe's cabin, and, depending on what she found, they may spend a few hours here. *Or not.*

She moved inside and throughout, finding it clean and empty. She'd stayed here a couple times herself. One larger bedroom was on the ground floor with a big double bed. She figured Rebecca and Becky could both go in there. Gemma would take the small bedroom at the back, so she could stay near her sister and her niece. No need to access the master bedroom suite on the second floor.

She walked back to the car, gently dragged the blankets

with the bundle containing Becky into her arms, then carried her into the cabin and put her on one side of the double bed. Rebecca came stumbling past her and crashed down beside her daughter. Tucking up against the little girl, she said, "I sure hope you think it's worth all this."

"Me too." She grabbed another blanket from the closet, tossed it over both of them and then headed out to the car. She grabbed a few personal things, like her laptop and her phone, and the burner phone Rebecca had left on the floor. Of all the things that pissed off her baby sister the most, losing her real phone was it. Gemma shook her head at her sister's lack of proper priorities. Heading back into the kitchen, she brought along the one bag of food she had. She put it on the counter, and, knowing she needed sleep more than anything, walked into the back bedroom and laid down on the small single cot near her sister and niece, closing her eyes. Almost immediately the burner phone buzzed. She looked at it to see a text from Zack, asking if they made it.

She responded, writing, **Yeah. Crashing for a few hours.**

We'll be there by the time you wake up.

She closed her eyes and whispered, "I hope not." But, on the inside, she wished she had some help with this. She had always been a very analytical person, and nothing about this whole scenario made any sense. The fact that her brother-in-law was dead was just one of those things that had to be dealt with. Her sister would need support and someone to stand at her side. Gemma didn't know what the hell was going on with Zack, or why he and Rebecca had walked away from each other all those years ago, but that wasn't Gemma's problem. That was theirs.

As she drifted off into slumber, her last thought was

wondering who the hell this Galen guy was. Was he the same caliber of guy as Zack? Would Galen have left his pregnant girlfriend too? She wouldn't judge all men by that one incident, but Zack had left a bad taste in her mouth. This Galen on the other hand? Something about his voice, with that crisp and clear commanding tone, had her smiling. She just hoped that it wasn't wrong to trust him. She had trusted the wrong people in the past and had gotten into deep shit. The last thing she wanted was more of that.

She closed her eyes and dozed, but she surfaced constantly. Asleep, awake; asleep, awake. Anytime she was about to go under, any odd noise outside had her lying here, wide awake, her ears tuned to see if more came. But, so far, all was quiet.

When she heard a vehicle drive up, she immediately hopped to her feet, walked out of the back bedroom into the main room, and peered behind the curtains of the living room window. She didn't recognize the small pickup, but she definitely recognized Zack's face in the windshield. She studied the guy beside him, realizing he sat both taller and wider. But he had the same kind of look to him.

As Zack stepped out, she frowned, not even recognizing the man in many ways. The years obviously hadn't been easy for him. He had changed. Maybe that was a good thing. He'd been one of her sister's conquests. For some reason Gemma had initially trusted him, even as she had worried about her sister's influence on him. Still, Rebecca had called him after all these years. When Rebecca broke up with Zack, Gemma had heard he'd gone into the military. Hence he might have skills to help her—them—out.

She let herself out the front door, then walked around the veranda to where they'd parked. Zack looked up at her.

"Are they okay?"

She nodded. "They are."

Galen hopped out, held out a hand, and said, "I'm Galen Alrick."

She shook his hand, looked at him, and frowned.

His eyebrows shot up. "Why the frown?"

"You look like you're used to taking charge," she said.

"I am." His voice sounded a challenge. "If a situation goes to shit, somebody has to."

"But that somebody should have been Zack a while ago," she snapped. "He didn't, so I did."

"If the situation is as bad as you made it out to be," Galen said with a nod, "then you did the right thing."

Almost immediately she could feel something settling inside her. And how sad was that? To think that some stranger gives her a note of approval, and here she was ready to smile and to accept him for it. "Maybe," she said. "I guess that will remain to be seen."

"Yep," he said. "Let's go in and talk."

"I don't think we have time," she said, glancing at her watch. "I think it's more important that we get on the road again."

"Are they awake?" Zack asked.

"Hold on," Galen said to her, his voice inflexible. He nodded toward Zack, already heading into the cabin. "Apparently he wants to make sure that Rebecca's here."

"Of course he does," she said, crossing her arms. "If there was ever a convoluted relationship, it is definitely theirs."

Galen chuckled. "I'm a simple guy," he said. "I like things up-front, clean, and honest.

"So do I," she said. "Yet people say that but then don't

necessarily follow through."

"I agree with you there." Taking the front steps two at a time, he stretched, rolling his neck. "Did you bring any coffee?"

"I don't want to take the time to put any on."

He nodded. "You really think they'll follow you here?"

"I'm counting on it," she said.

Picking up on her wording, he studied her intently. "Good. I'd like to hear about your plans. Can I presume you're leaving something for them to find?"

She shrugged. "Hopefully just enough. It's what *I* want to find that's the purpose for being here."

"What are you thinking of?"

She frowned. "How are you with electronics?"

He gave her a long, slow smile. "Decent. Have you any experience with them?"

"I have," she said. "It just depends on whether I can make things work or not."

"Come on in. Let's talk." He opened the door and motioned at her.

As they walked in, Zack was putting on coffee with Rebecca at his side.

GALEN STUDIED ZACK, wondering what was going on. Rebecca and Zack looked friendly enough but not close.

Good.

But Zack's face was shut down, focused on what he was doing, which, thankfully, was putting on coffee. However, Gemma didn't appear to be too impressed with that.

"I don't want to stay here long," Gemma reiterated.

"We have time for coffee," Zack said. "You brought the

stuff. We might as well use it."

"I did," she said, "and I was of two minds, but I wanted to leave soon."

"It's normal for anybody to walk in and put on coffee," Zack said. "Are there cups here, or did you bring some?"

Gemma shook her head. "No, I meant to pick some up but forgot. We can check the cupboards."

"Coffee just says we were here long enough to sit and relax," he said smoothly. "So that isn't an issue."

Galen watched the back-and-forth between them as the conversation wrangled. Obviously some hard feelings were between them, but that wasn't Galen's problem. He looked at Rebecca to see her now slumped in a chair, rubbing the sleep from her eyes. Emerald eyes and red hair and a body that screamed of sex. The complete opposite to Gemma's huge soft gray eyes framed by long lashes that only emphasized the direct look in her gaze and a body that demanded love, honesty, trust. Long and lean, she was more racehorse than model. And he already knew which he preferred.

"You need to tell us what's going on." Galen spoke quietly as he walked toward Rebecca.

She snorted and looked up at her sister. "Talk to her. Nobody else can say anything."

"Meaning?"

"Meaning, I'm here against my will," she snapped, then let out a heavy sigh.

"Give it a rest, Rebecca," Gemma said.

"Why should I?" she snapped. "Everything you're talking about is complete BS. It's typical older-sister crap, and I'm tired of it." She glared at her sister.

Gemma walked out of the kitchen, through the living room, and exited the front door.

Galen looked at Rebecca with interest. "And what is it that she thinks?"

"She says Joe was murdered." Her words were emphasized with a wave of her right hand. "The cops made it clear that it was a burglary gone wrong. Gemma always has to escalate things."

"And why is that?" he asked, as he stared at the empty doorway the older sister had left through. The look on Gemma's face had suggested she'd heard it all time and time again.

"Because she feels responsible that she couldn't stop the death of our parents," she said with a frustrated sigh. "And she's looked after me since I was fifteen. But I don't need looking after anymore."

"Well, maybe you should reassess that." Zack's voice was hard and determined. "Because Joe *was* murdered."

Chapter 3

G EMMA HEARD HER sister's verbal explosion after Zack's words, but Gemma was too tired to go back inside and do anything. As she stared out into the landscape from the front veranda, she could feel the stress and strain of making all the decisions for the last couple days. She knew that she had to, otherwise it would be the end of her sister and potentially her little niece, whose life didn't deserve to be cut short because Joe had been an honest and upstanding citizen.

Gemma had really liked Joe. He'd been good for Rebecca—a calm and steady partner. They had seemed happy together. Zack had been a flash in the pan years ago. He still didn't look like he was right for her, but that was her sister's choice. In the meantime, Gemma had done what she thought was right. Sometimes making the hard decisions made her very unpopular.

She could hear them talking in the front room and knew that she should join the conversation, as much as she didn't want to. She felt vindicated that Zack had agreed with her assessment of Joe's death. But they still didn't know all the details. She doubted her sister would think to bring it up. In some ways Rebecca was an airhead. In other ways, she was a good mother.

When a hand settled on her shoulder, gentle but firm, she had been startled but didn't turn around. She instinctively knew it was Galen.

"You were right, you know."

She nodded but didn't say anything.

"What I'd like to know is what caused you to pick up and run."

"At midnight a couple nights ago somebody tried to break into the house. I chased him away, and I had set up a security system of sorts, so he would set it off and wake us up. But I'm not very good at it," she said. "It was just a case of dishes and a chair jammed under the door. So when he came again around one a.m., I heard him once more, but he heard the commotion he was making and took off." She twisted slightly to look up at Galen. "I could see his profile. I know it was the same guy both times."

"Could you describe him?"

"I told the police, but they weren't too interested. They said it was likely just a neighborhood kid."

"Did they take down your details?"

"Yeah, they did," she said, reaching up to cover a yawn. "Not that it made any difference."

"Did the cops come to the house?"

She nodded. "Yes, but they wouldn't find anything. He wore gloves. I could see that clearly too. He had on a plaid flannel jacket with a bright colored lining. Orange, I think." She was very tired; it came out in her words. "Jeans and some kind of heavy work boots."

"That's still a lot of detail."

"Motion sensor lights are outside Rebecca's house," she said, "and he stepped into one."

"Which meant he also hadn't scouted out the place beforehand."

"He was much quieter the second time. At least outside."

She nodded, as if agreeing with herself. "But a different light reflection caught him." She shrugged. "I figured he came twice, and he probably wouldn't fail the third time."

"And you think it's related to Joe?"

She hesitated, and he squeezed her shoulder.

"Why?"

"Because I think I saw our intruder with Joe in the past," she said quietly. "Joe was involved in a heavy investigation at the brewery after several break-ins before he was killed. He made a lot of changes at work, and many accusations were flung around, but I don't know that anyone was charged. I don't know any of the details, but it seemed like it was much better for everybody if Joe wasn't around. He was a nice guy but a stickler for rules and loved to make even more. He also wouldn't allow any break-ins on his watch. I think he thought those were connected to supporters of his predecessor."

"From what I've heard, that would make sense," he said, "and that fits with him being murdered. But what possible reason could they have for wiping out his wife and daughter?"

"Just in case Joe said anything to them, maybe? In case he hid anything? I don't know. Many answers probably fit that question."

"Would he have?" Galen asked. "Would he discuss that with Rebecca?" His frown said no.

Gemma shook her head. "I have no idea. Probably not."

"But Joe could have hidden something, from his investigation into his predecessor that lost him his job?"

Gemma nodded. "Quite possibly, yes," she said. "Yeah. I could definitely see him doing that. He was a methodical guy. If he saw discrepancies in the brewery's systems, wherever, Joe would have spoken up."

"Tell me about seeing this guy with Joe."

"There was a big summer barbecue last year," she said. "I was visiting my sister in between a couple business trips, and we all went to the big bash. I'm pretty sure I saw him then."

"So it could have been anybody associated with the company or with the extended family?"

"Or a visitor like me, yes," she said.

"Well, your position was unique, in that you were extended family and a visitor, right?" he asked for clarification.

"Yes. I'm sure the event was supposed to be just for immediate family."

"How big of a company did Joe work for?"

"It's one of the major breweries in Germany, in the world, I guess. But his local manufacturing plant entailed about a hundred and forty employees, I think," she answered. "I went to the website and tried to see if they had photos. I do a lot of computer work myself, but I didn't hack into the system. I tried though."

He looked at her sharply, and she gave him a flat look.

"Hey, I've had to do a lot to look after my sister and my niece, to keep them alive," she said. "We lost our parents years ago, and I've been looking after her since then."

"Sounds like you've had your hands full."

"You have no idea," she said with a short laugh.

"She would have been what, fifteen or so?" Galen asked.

"Just turned fifteen," she said. "Our parents died in a car accident two days after her birthday."

"Surely you don't feel guilty for that somehow, do you?"

"Yes, but no."

He waited for her to explain, his eyebrows raised expectantly.

She sighed. "They were coming to pick me up. I was at a play rehearsal, and I got sick. I didn't want to be there or have anything to do with it in the first place, but they had insisted. While I was there, I got really nervous and started throwing up," she said honestly. "I called and told them how I couldn't do it, and they were coming to pick me up when the accident occurred."

"Ouch," he said. "But still, not your fault."

"No, but it was in a way," she said, "and you can bet my sister never let me forget it."

"That's not true," Rebecca said from the doorway. "At least I didn't mean for you to feel that way."

"For years," Gemma said, surprised that her sister was there, "you threw it in my face, saying how they'd be alive if it wasn't for me."

"I didn't mean it though," she said. "I was a mixed-up teenager."

"You think?" Gemma walked toward Rebecca, hands shoved in her pockets, frowning at her. "Looking after you hasn't been easy, you know?"

"Because you were supposed to stop looking after me," she argued, "like eight, nine years ago."

"When you came to me pregnant?" Gemma asked. "Or when you were wondering aloud if you should marry Joe because you wanted some security?"

Zack stood behind Rebecca at the open doorway, easily hearing everything.

At that, Rebecca had the grace to look ashamed. "Okay, I guess I have been a trial to you, haven't I?"

Gemma shrugged her shoulders irritably, the rehash of their history never pleasant. "It is what it is. You haven't been easy to look after, but that's all water under the bridge now." Gemma gave her a forced bright smile and turned away.

"Hardly," Rebecca said. An awkward silence ensued as the four of them looked at each other. "Zack says Joe was murdered."

"Right, so because Zack said it, you believe it now?" Gemma asked in outrage. "Even though that's exactly what I've been telling you this whole time?"

"Yes, but you didn't have any reason why."

"Right. If you say so." Gemma turned to face the guys. "If we're not leaving right away, which I think is the wrong thing to do, I'll go lie down and get some rest while I can."

"I don't see why we had to leave my home at all," Rebecca replied.

"Because someone tried to break in twice two nights ago. And he will come here next," she said with a tired sigh. "Just ask the men. They already know it." She listened as her sister turned to Zack.

"Are they?"

"Yes," he said quietly, "they will come here."

Just as Gemma headed to the small rear bedroom, Galen called out, "What was your plan after this?"

She turned and looked at him. "I've rented a cabin not very far from here," she said, "with the idea that we could blend into that area."

"What kind of a cabin?"

She gave him a ghostly smile. "It's kind of a hippie colony," she said. "They have a couple cabins they rent out for extra money."

"You don't think we'll stick out like a sore thumb there?" Rebecca cried out in shock.

"I said a hippie colony, not a back-to-square-roots type

thing. They have internet and computers."

"It's not a bad idea." Zack nodded. "Depends if anybody can track the transaction?"

"They only do cash, and I arranged it a long time ago," she said.

"Why?" Galen asked, curious.

"Because, once Joe started down this pathway at work, it looked to me like he was heading into trouble. I tried to talk him out of it for Rebecca's sake, but he said he had to do what was right and that he'd try his best to keep her safe in the meantime."

"I never knew you did that," her sister said, staring at her in shock. "He never said anything to me about it."

"He didn't say anything because you didn't want to hear anything," Gemma said in exasperation. "You haven't changed, Rebecca. You want what you want, and you don't want anybody telling you anything different or unpleasant ever." With a shake of her head, she sighed. "I'll try to get a quick nap. Then you guys can decide if you're coming with me or not." And, with that, she closed the door to her bedroom.

GALEN LOOKED AT Zack and grinned. "I like her."

Zack snorted. "You would. She's always been clear about right and wrong."

"Like how? It would be nice if someone around here liked me," Rebecca complained. "You like me, Zack, don't you?"

He nodded affectionately. "Yep, but I've known you for a decade."

"Right," she said sadly. "How come we didn't get together?"

"Don't know," he said cheerfully. "It just wasn't right for us."

"Maybe it is now," she said, looking at him thoughtfully.

Galen was interested to see Zack's reaction. He just shook his head. Galen still didn't understand their relationship, but he'd choose Gemma over Rebecca any day. Hell, he'd love to spend some time to get to know Gemma better.

"You're the little sister I never had," Zack said. "We'll keep it at that."

She nodded glumly. "I wish Joe wasn't dead."

Galen had to admit he didn't think she cared about Joe being gone because she loved and missed him but more that he'd been there looking after her and now she didn't know what to do. She had pretty much alienated her sister from what he could see. The relationship definitely wasn't one of mutual decision-making. And, for that, he felt sorry for Joe.

He looked at Zack to see a similar look of mixed emotions on Zack's face. Galen finally realized that the answer to what he'd been wondering—if Rebecca was the one for Zack—was no. It really was a past relationship, and she'd slid into the kid-sister slot in Zack's life. Which would make this job a lot easier.

Zack looked at him. "So what do you think?"

"I think Gemma's right," he said. "The fact that she found a couple places to rent is also unique. She's very proactive." Zack nodded, as Galen continued, "And maybe you didn't hear, but she asked for my help. She said potentially some electronics were here."

At that, Zack's eyebrows rose. He looked at the closed door of the bedroom and nodded. "She's always been one step ahead of the others."

"And, in this case at least, she's doing it for all the right reasons."

Rebecca crossed her arms over her chest and glared at the men. "I'm right here, though I'm not sure I understand what you're talking about."

"Doesn't matter," Zack said, wrapping an arm around her shoulder, giving her a quick hug. He looked at Galen. "We should check the car for the stuff then."

They headed outside, leaving Gemma to get some sleep while they went to the car. They took a look at the stuff in the trunk.

Rebecca came with the guys to the car. "Becky should be waking up soon, and I'll need a hell of an explanation ready for this," she announced.

"Why?" Galen asked.

"She had a party to go to this weekend, and she'll be pretty upset to miss it."

Galen nodded. He figured a little girl would get over it, but there might be some tears first. "So whose car is this?" he asked Rebecca.

"Whoever gave her the car is a secret, so don't ask. She won't even tell me who it was." Rebecca's tone held resentment. "He also gave her cash."

"Cash is good," Galen said mildly, noting the visible disgust on Rebecca's face.

As they dug into the trunk of the car, she grabbed two bags. "These are Becky's."

He looked at them, nodded, looked at the rest of the gear in the back of the car, and asked, "So how much of this is yours?"

She pointed out six suitcases.

Six. He looked at her. "And this was a quick pack for

you?"

She shrugged. "I didn't know what I would need, did I?" And, with that, she sauntered inside.

He looked at Zack. "Only one suitcase in here she didn't point to."

Zack nodded slowly. "Yeah, that'll be Gemma's." He shook his head and pointed to a box. "What's in there?"

Sure enough, it was electronics. Computerized electronics with long-life batteries.

"This is pretty sophisticated stuff." Galen whistled. "And this hooks up to the satellite feed."

"Let's get this inside, and see what we can do," Zack said. It didn't take long to sort out that she had three security cameras. "One front, one back?"

"Maybe one inside for close-ups?"

As Gemma came out the bedroom door, she nodded, rubbing her eyes.

He frowned at her. "You weren't down for very long."

"I do power naps," she said. "I just have to go down, and then I'm good after ten minutes." She noted the absence of her sister. "Is Rebecca in with Becky?" she asked, pointing at another closed door.

"Yeah," Zack confirmed.

Gemma motioned at the box. "So that is all I have. Except for my laptop which connects to these."

"Did you try them?"

"I did, which is why I'm short on sleep."

The guys nodded, bringing the rest of the stuff inside the cabin. She brought out her laptop from a huge bag he'd noticed sitting off to the side in the kitchen area. One of those over-the-shoulder purses which women carried around that seemed to hold everything. And, sure enough, she pulled out a modem, several battery packs, a mouse, and then a notebook.

She sat down at the small kitchen table and quickly turned on the laptop. "My thoughts had been one for the front road, one for the back door, and one for inside somewhere along this transition wall." She pointed up to where the wall was. "We could then potentially see the kitchen and living room and somebody coming up and down the stairs."

With that agreement in place, the men quickly secured the cameras as best they could to be out of the way, hidden, even bringing some greenery in to make it look like it was a decoration.

With that set up, she brought up the software and motioned to the computer. "Numbers one and two are online."

Galen stepped behind her to take a look. "Good enough. Number three isn't picking up anything though." He walked over and readjusted it. "I don't like the looks of the sensor in the back."

She went to a box and brought out a smaller box from inside. "Here. These are replacement sensors."

He looked at them in surprise. "Where did you get this stuff?"

"I have connections."

He grinned at that. "So do I," he said, with an approving nod. "They're good to have." He could feel more easing of her stiffness.

She nodded. "They've been a saving grace so far."

"That's how you got the car?"

"How do you know it's not mine?"

"I checked."

"Hell, yes, that's how I got the car."

He was glad that Gemma had somebody capable of helping her right now. He wished that he'd been the one she called. Something was just so compelling about that quiet take-charge way about her, to the point that he was getting irritated with the sister and would like to just ditch her. But that was hardly the point, when keeping her safe was why they were here in the first place. "What about at Joe's home?"

"Three," Gemma said quietly.

He smiled. "Different system I presume?"

"Yes, and different software. The software has some glitchy crap that keeps throwing me."

"But you're in IT, right?"

"Medical systems," she said. "But honestly, the security in the back end of many of these big systems is similar."

"I've heard that," he said. "Not sure I've seen any medical systems to know though."

"Nothing really to look at," she said. "Take a look at any banking system, and you'll find something similar."

"Ah, they're all built on the same backbone, aren't they?"

"They are," she said. She switched off several other screens and brought up the house.

He watched as she connected to all three of them. "How long does it hold the feed?"

"I've got it running for two days right now," she said. "I'm hoping that we can check on it at a regular basis, but I don't know how steady the internet will be for that kind of access."

"Can you get it longer?"

"I'm hoping to," she said. "I'd like at least four days, but I haven't been able to get it to work. It keeps glitching out when I try to save the new settings."

"Mind if I try?" he asked.

She hopped up and took a step back. "Be my guest."

"What is this?" Rebecca asked, coming out of the bigger bedroom and up behind them. "That's my house," she snapped. She turned to glare at her sister. "Have you been watching me?"

"Oh, for God's sake," Gemma said, "I set it up so we could see if anybody goes through the house now that we're gone."

"Well, somebody did," Galen said, pointing out the cops.

"I know, but that was before. And then Zack went through. And that's how you called me, I presume?" she said to him.

Zack nodded. "But I didn't see the cameras, so that was a nice job, Gemma."

"You weren't looking for them," she said.

"You're right. I wasn't. And, once I realized that Rebecca's personal cell phone was still there, I knew something bad had happened."

"Of course." Rebecca turned on her sister. "I told you that he would."

"I was counting on it," Gemma said calmly. "I hope you came armed?"

"We both are," Zack said with understanding. "So you wanted us to follow you?"

"Just like you wanted Galen for backup," she said, "I needed backup too."

Just then a faint cry came from the bedroom. "Mommy?"

Chapter 4

GEMMA SMILED WHEN she heard Becky's voice. Rebecca headed toward the bedroom, calling out, "It's okay, sweetie. Mom's here."

Gemma looked at Zack to see his gaze following her sister. "You never did find out, did you?"

He shrugged. "Not for certain. No."

"You may want to," she said. "At least then you could possibly cut that tie."

"No," he said, shaking his head. "It's probably better if I don't."

Gemma left it at that, but Rebecca had always refused to say who Becky's father was. Gemma had assumed Zack stayed in contact, wondering if he was. She wasn't sure she wanted to make it an issue. Some things had to be left to her sister to sort out for herself. Although, for the most part, that never seemed to happen.

Just then Rebecca came out with Becky in her arms, wrapped up in a blanket. Becky was small framed and more doll-like than most girls. The minute Becky saw Zack, she curled deeper into her mother's arms. When she saw Gemma, she grinned, opening her arms. Gemma walked over, took her niece from her mother's arms, and cuddled her close.

Rebecca sighed and stared at the two of them. "I still

don't understand that," she said, throwing the blanket over her arm, while she pouted and headed back into the bedroom. "She doesn't see you for months. Then the two of you are like that." And she snapped her fingers.

"Hey, how's my girl?" Gemma murmured.

"I'm fine," she said. "Mom said you made us come here."

Gemma chuckled. "You could say that," she said, "but we're heading to a farm next. We're leaving here any minute."

"A farm?" Becky said, sitting up to look at her aunt. "What kind of farm?"

"With big gardens, chickens and ducks, dogs, kitties and all kinds of things," she promised.

Becky beamed, her arms wrapped around her aunt. "Okay." And then, as if suddenly aware of another person in the room, she turned and stared at Galen. "Who are you?" she asked bluntly.

"Zack's friend," he said.

"And," Gemma added quietly, "a friend of mine."

Becky immediately let her emotions be known. "Good," she said. "Then you're fine."

GALEN WATCHED THE interaction between the little girl and Gemma. Becky seemed almost more comfortable with Gemma than with her own mother. But her mother appeared to be a spoiled brat, so he could certainly understand preferring the calm, level-headed, unflappable aunt Becky could depend on. He certainly did. And the fact that her aunt had given him the stamp of approval made it all okay in the little girl's eyes.

He wondered what kind of a life Becky had with her mother. Obviously Joe had been a great influence, so how had his death affected her? Had she been allowed to grieve and to still talk about her father, or was she supposed to keep him out of her life now that he was gone? People handled death differently, but little children especially processed things in a very different way than adults. Sometimes they needed to constantly talk about the father, or the deceased one, in order to still be comfortably connected with them.

As it was, Gemma was already making a move to pack up the few things they'd unpacked, even with the little girl in her arms.

"I'm hungry," Becky said.

"Of course you are," Gemma said affectionately. "You're always hungry."

"I'm growing," she said. "Soon I'll be as big as you."

"I hope not," Gemma said. "Maybe you'll be somewhere between your mom and me."

But the little girl was having nothing to do with it. "Nope. I'll be tall. Daddy was tall, so I'll be tall."

Gemma nodded nonchalantly as Galen watched. This was either a conversation she'd had many times or else she was completely comfortable with the discussion. He looked over at Zack, who studied the little girl, and Galen wondered if Zack, Joe, and Rebecca had been in some sort of a love triangle, if that's what was going on. It would be sad if it was. Or maybe not, if Zack decided to take a step forward now. But it didn't look like that's where his heart lay.

Galen looked to Gemma. "Did you want to do food now?" he asked.

She nodded. "Yeah, I was hoping to get moved on first, but that won't happen now."

Immediately Becky shook her head. "Nope. I'm starving now."

Gemma put her niece down on the top of the counter and dug into the box of food sitting beside Becky. "I brought eggs and bread for toast. How about an egg sandwich?"

"Okay," she said. "Do you have ham or bacon?"

"I have ham, but we need it for sandwiches later."

The little girl's face wrinkled up as she thought about it; then she nodded. "Eggs will do."

Gemma chuckled. "Thank you for that royal decree, little princess."

And, with that, the little girl went off in peals of laughter.

While Gemma settled Becky on the floor, so Gemma could make sandwiches—enough for everybody it seemed—Galen walked outside to check the layout of the land. He'd already brought up on his phone the next place she had booked and approved of it in many ways. They would blend in nicely, as long as nobody there said anything. He wondered if she had friends at the compound or if this was a connection that came through her other friends, like those who had arranged for the electronics or the car. How else would anybody know the compound was there?

Zack came up beside him. "I don't know how long we'll stay in the next place."

"What we don't want to do is keep running," Galen said. "There's got to be another answer."

"Yeah, find out who killed Joe."

"I get that," he said. "I'm surprised she thinks they'll come here though."

"Well, Joe talked about this cabin quite a bit."

"So then she's thinking they probably already checked it

out?"

"I would have," he said, "and you know you would have too."

While she continued to make sandwiches, the guys packed up the rest of the stuff, loading the trunk again. When they walked back inside, he noted a big platter full of sandwiches. She must have made at least a dozen of them. He looked at her, surprised.

She shrugged. "It's much easier to make them with scrambled eggs if you have to do a lot of them. Eat up."

He nodded and reached for a half sandwich and was surprised at how good it tasted. By the time they'd eaten, and she'd washed everything and put away the kitchenware, the place looked like nobody had been here. But he also knew that anybody remotely like himself would find signs otherwise.

She walked through to the single bedroom and then the bigger bedroom on the first floor, checked both over, before walking upstairs to the master suite.

He followed, keeping an eye on her until she returned to the first floor. "Where did you learn to do this?"

She gave him a shuttered look and shrugged. "Let's just say I have friends."

"Sounds like you have a lot of interesting friends."

"I do," she said, "but that doesn't change the fact that they aren't necessarily people you call on all the time."

He nodded. "Have they helped you out in the past?"

"Sometimes, yes. I met them in school, and years ago a group of them went one way, and the rest of the world went the other," she said with a laugh. "They've always stayed on the fringe side." She looked around again. "Come on. Let's go."

Galen let her lead the way outside. They all got into the two vehicles, Galen and Zack following her and Rebecca and Becky to the next place Gemma had booked. This one was a bit farther than a few miles down the road, and he was glad to see the route also went onto the main highway. So any tracks they left behind would blend in with the rest of the traffic.

She took a turn up ahead onto a long gravel road with no signage. She drove slowly, and they followed it as she missed a bunch of the potholes, and yet continued into the rutted driveway that got worse the farther in they went.

Zack looked at him in surprise. "Wonder how the hell she found out about this place."

"She said something about having friends."

"Mysterious."

"You've obviously known her for a long time," Galen said.

"Not her. She's never been one anybody got to know," he said. "She has always been mysterious."

"I kind of like that," Galen said with a laugh.

"Maybe," Zack said. "Sounds like she likes you better than me anyway."

"Any reason for that?"

"No, I don't think so," Zack said, settling back. "I haven't had too much to do with the family for the last eight years."

"Is Becky yours?"

A strange silence filled in the vehicle, and finally Zack looked at him. "No."

"Good enough," Galen said, wondering at the slowness of his partner's response.

"Why would you ask me that?" Zack asked.

"A definite undercurrent was going on around the place."

"Let's just say, Rebecca and I had a relationship when she had an affair with Joe," he said.

"Ouch," Galen said. "So then, for a while, you wouldn't have known who the father was."

"I knew it wasn't me," Zack said. "Every once in a while though I look at Becky and wonder," he admitted.

"And did you want more?"

"Back then, yes, when I was young and idealistic, and Rebecca was pretty, but I didn't know she was seeing someone else at the same time. Now, not so much."

"She seems like the kind who needs to have a guy around her," Galen said. "If not multiples."

"Yep, and she doesn't understand her sister for not having that," Zack said.

"Interesting."

Just then, the vehicle in front of them took a sharp turn onto what was barely a road. But Galen was driving this time, and he took the same turn. "You know something? If it were anybody else, no way we would go down this road alone."

"I was just thinking that," Zack said, sitting forward. "Why don't you stop here, and I'll get out."

Galen eased off to the side slightly and slowed down. Zack quickly bailed, and Galen kept on going, hoping that the two women in front hadn't seen Zack's disappearance. Galen wasn't sure what was going on, but, as they came around the corner, he saw a homestead with multiple houses and buildings, plus outbuildings and animals. All the animals Gemma had promised Becky. He knew the little girl would love it.

Her vehicle pulled up to one side where a large SUV was parked. Even though she hadn't driven that far, Gemma got out and stretched like a feline. Becky bailed out the other side, running to find the animals.

"Stop!" Gemma called out to her.

The little girl struggled to comply, but she did stop.

Galen had to wonder what the child's response would have been if her mother had called out instead. It was like Gemma's word was law.

Gemma walked over and reached out her hand. Putting hers in it, Becky peppered Gemma with a million questions.

Rebecca got out and stood behind them, resentful as always.

Galen wondered at the relationship between the three of them, but he quickly caught up with Rebecca, who glared at him and asked, "Where's Zack?"

"He's coming," he replied. "Don't you want to catch up with the other two?"

"I just want to go home," she snapped. "I'm not the countrified bumpkin that my sister is."

"Is she country?" He turned to look at the tall woman in front of them, walking with calm, sure strides toward a long low building, as if she knew exactly where she was going.

"She's everything she always wanted to be, and she changes like a chameleon," Rebecca whined.

"Are the two of you very different?"

"Yes, we are. Very different. It's as if we had different parents, yet didn't."

He nodded. "Genetics are wondrous things."

"Or not. She's always been on my case," Rebecca said. "I know sometimes I sound ungrateful and unappreciative of all she's done, but it's been really hard having her as an older sister."

He wasn't sure if this was just normal bitching and whining or if Rebecca had some actual beef with some merit from their past. "Has she ever done anything to hurt you?"

"No," Rebecca said. "It would be nice if she had. But, no, she's always been so uber-responsible that it's sickening."

"And you, of course, you've been the uber-rebellious one, huh?"

At that, she laughed and smiled. "Well, I always felt like there should be more to life than simply duty." She pointed at Gemma. "She's always been the one who did the right thing. And sometimes I just got so tired of it that I felt I had to rebel just to be me."

"That's understandable," he said. "Do you know the people here?"

"God, no," she said. "How would I?"

"I don't know," Galen said. "I just wondered if maybe they were family friends or something."

"No. I can assure you that I wouldn't know anybody who lived in a place like this. The lifestyle I had with Joe was perfect. We had a lot of evenings out, were on a lot of committees and boards," she said. "Sunday brunches out with the ladies' golf group, not that I could play, but I could certainly sit there afterward and have a drink or two."

"So, you were all set, settled into the perfect life."

"We were well on our way to it," she said resentfully. "I still can't believe Joe's dead."

"I'm sorry," he said. "It must have been tough."

She stared at him. "I don't think it's really sunk in, actually." Her words came out quietly, for once losing the resentful-child outer image that she seemed to wear like a mantle. "He was also uber-responsible."

"So next time you find somebody," he said, "maybe you'll pick someone who will actually spend time with you and not just look after you."

She stared at him in surprise.

He gave her a half smile. "Choose someone you want, not someone you think you should have." When he heard a call, he turned to see Gemma standing on the front deck of a nearby building, motioning them to come over. He reached down and gently nudged Rebecca's elbow. "Come on. They want us to join them."

"Of course they do," she said with an unhappy sigh. Then she announced, "I'll be absolutely miserable here for a few days."

"If you want to be miserable, you will be," he said.

She turned and glared at him.

He shrugged. "Or you could choose something different and make this a fun time for your daughter to enjoy."

"She'll enjoy it anyway because she'll be with her favorite perfect person," she snapped.

With that, she strode off ahead, leaving him with an ugly impression of much worse than just resentment in the family. He hoped it was only on the surface and didn't impact the safety of the three of them because that would be hard to forgive. But he had to wonder just how deep Rebecca's resentment went.

Chapter 5

GEMMA STUDIED HER sister's face as she approached. Rebecca looked the same as always—put upon and upset. Like everything was a grand inconvenience. Hopefully Rebecca was hiding deeper feelings of worry over Joe's demise, but Gemma never could be sure. Her sister had always seemed very superficial. Gemma knew there had to be feelings deep inside, but it appeared that Rebecca neither took the time nor allowed herself to feel them.

Finally she hopped up onto the deck beside them. Gemma smiled and said, "We'll go in and say hello, and then I'll take you to the rooms. I'm sure everybody could use a break by now."

Immediately Becky shook her head. "I want to see the animals!"

"Maybe," Gemma temporized. "But don't forget we need permission first, so you have to be on your best behavior."

Becky immediately nodded and smiled. "I will be."

Gemma looked at her sister. "You too."

She shot her look. "I'm not a child."

Frustrated, Gemma didn't say anything as Galen approached just then. Gemma walked into what appeared to be an office, and everybody followed.

There, a single man stood behind a small desk doing

some paperwork. He looked up and smiled. "You must be our guests."

Gemma smiled and nodded. "We're here for a couple days."

"Welcome." He looked at Becky. "Was it you I heard who wanted to see the animals?"

Becky beamed. "Yes. Please," she added.

"Once we get you settled into your cabin," he said, "we can do that." He turned behind him and reached for two keys hanging on separate hooks. "I'll show you where you'll be staying." With that, he walked past the small group, out the door, and turned left.

They followed behind him. Gemma had been here before, many times as a child and a teenager, and had stayed in touch with the group who owned the place. She knew Galen and Zack were curious about her friendships, but she kept them in the dark on purpose. Her friends preferred it that way, and, since she'd known them for so long and had accepted them for who they were, she didn't have a problem with that. Lots of people did though. They took a group of individuals like this who liked to live on the edge of society and tore them apart mentally, trying to figure out what made them tick and whether they were loose time bombs or not. She was just happy to let them be themselves.

As she walked along, she asked, "How has the year treated you, Tim?"

Galen noted that the man hadn't introduced himself.

Tim looked at her, smiled, and commented, "It's been good. The crops have been prolific. The animals have been decent. We've got two more babies in the group," he said proudly. "We're all happy. That's what counts."

She nodded and didn't say anything more. He opened

up the first cabin, and she stepped inside and smiled. She was always okay with the simple life. She knew her sister would freak out though.

They walked to the second cabin which was a little bigger and had a bedroom in the back.

"This is where you two will stay, Becky," she said, turning to look at her sister. "I figured Zack can stay in here with you."

Rebecca stared at her, surprised. "And you?"

"I'll stay at the other one," she said.

Rebecca pinched her lips together, as she contemplated that and then shrugged. "Sure, I'll take the bedroom. Whatever."

"You and Becky," Gemma said firmly.

She sighed. "Of course, me and Becky. Why do you always see me in a bad light?"

"I don't," she said, "but I always see you as being you."

"And somehow *that* came across as very insulting," Rebecca snapped.

"Listen. I'm not trying to be difficult," Gemma said with a long-winded sigh. No matter what she said, her sister would take it as a criticism. She handed her sister the key. "This is the key to your cabin." She walked back over to hers and stepped inside to find Galen here. "I wasn't aware of you when I made these arrangements."

"I'm staying in here," he said firmly.

She studied him for a long moment, shrugged, and said, "That's fine." She could tell from the look on his face that she'd surprised him. "Did you expect a fight?"

"No," he said, "but I didn't expect you to give in so easily though."

"If trouble comes," she said, "I'll be glad to have you on

my side."

"Are you expecting trouble?"

"I don't know. I hope not," she said. "I really don't want to bring it to these quiet folks around us."

"So, are we putting up guards overnight?" he asked.

"I was planning on it," she said. "I do need some sleep though."

"Some sleep?"

"I'm one of those weirdos who don't sleep much," she said with a dismissive shrug. "Four hours is plenty for me."

"I need at least six," he said, studying her in an odd way.

But then she was used to that. Everybody thought she was odd, different, or unique, but usually just weird.

The two of them stood, comfortably staring at each other, and then he motioned outside and asked, "Now what?"

"Now," she said, "we need to check up on Joe's cabin that we just left, and on Joe's house, and see if anybody's been there."

Galen tilted his head. "You could leave that to us."

"I could," she said. "I've been around guys like you before. Some of them are good, and some of them aren't."

"That's like everybody in the world. So what do you mean when you say 'guys like us' anyway?"

She gave him a hard look. "My fiancé was ex-military."

"Ex-fiancé or ex-military?"

"Both."

"So you don't trust us anymore?"

"I trusted him implicitly—until I didn't trust him anymore."

"Sounds like a story in there. Are you always such an enigma?"

"Nothing's mysterious about me at all," she said with

surprise. "But when I love, I love deep. And when I'm loyal, I'm loyal forever. But apparently that's not the way the rest of the world is." With that, she turned and headed toward the front door.

"Gemma, did you have anything to do with Joe's death?"

She turned and looked at him in surprise. "Hell no," she said. "Joe was a good guy."

"So why do you think he was killed?"

"The easy answer is, he was killed entirely due to the mess he created at work with the changes he implemented. He also cut back the amount of free beer each employee could take home a month. That might have gotten him killed alone," she said with a small smile. "But he wasn't easy to work with or to live with. In spite of that, I liked him. He was a simple person with very high ideals and expected the rest of the world to be the same. But this is just my guess. I don't know anything about that. It's only what I'm assuming."

"And your sister?"

Gemma stopped at that but made no pretense about not understanding. "I would like to think she had nothing to do with it. That's the premise I'm operating on. It would be devastating if she had. But I also think that, if she had, it would have only been to further her own purposes."

"Is she that selfish?"

"We're all selfish," Gemma said, "but, in her case, I wouldn't have thought she could be so incredibly selfish as to kill Joe."

GALEN WATCHED HER closely. "And why do you expect the

killer to come out this far?"

"Because, if they already killed once," she said in exasperation, "what's to stop them from killing again? I would do a lot to keep my niece alive."

"And your sister?"

"I've already done a lot to keep her alive," she said sadly, "but my sister has a mind of her own and doesn't always listen to what's best for her."

Just then a voice from outside the cabin door snapped, "You mean, what *you* think is best for her."

Gemma waved her hand. "Let's take Becky to see the animals," she said. "It'll keep her happy for a while."

"True enough," Rebecca said, giving in, but still glaring at her sister, as if this were an old argument with no winners.

Galen watched as the women immediately joined forces for the little girl's happiness and headed off to look at the animals. He, on the other hand, did a quick sweep of the cabin and then pulled out his laptop, connected up to the surveillance equipment they had left at Joe's cabin and to Joe and Rebecca's house. As he went through the videos, he couldn't see any unwelcome guests, which made him feel marginally better. Also a part of him said this whole thing was a wild goose chase and completely unnecessary, but, for whatever reason, Gemma seemed to think it wasn't, and she definitely wasn't the kind to flap over nothing.

As he stepped out the front door, he heard a short whistle. He turned to look at Zack, motioning at him from the other cabin. Galen walked over and joined him on the front deck, where there were two chairs. "So, what did you learn?" Galen asked.

"I checked out the compound. They are pretty heavily armed."

He turned slowly and stared at Zack. "Seriously?"

Zack nodded. "There's a full armory, and I'm talking AK-47s and hand grenades. That level of armed."

"Do you think Gemma knows?"

"I wouldn't be surprised either way."

"I don't think it would bother her if she doesn't," Galen said. "Something about her makes me think she's completely okay with weapons. But I don't know if she expects her friends here to be quite that well armed."

"Or she was counting on it, and that's why we're here," Zack said.

"Good point. If so, it was smart of her again. That's possible too. I've checked the camera screens, and there's no activity I could see at Joe's cabin or the house."

"No?" He scratched his head. "I'm not sure if that's good or bad at this point."

"I did get an update from Levi," Galen said. "Sounds like the police are looking to close the case as a burglary. Whereas they should be looking at it as yet another connected break-in to the brewery."

"Which would mean the murderer gets away scot-free," Zack said derisively, shaking his head. "The cops don't see this as connected."

"Possibly. But we need a witness or a weak link in this that we can put some pressure on, to see if we could blow things up a bit."

"I think the weak link is here," he said. "I'm pretty sure Rebecca knows more than she's saying."

Galen looked at Zack, surprised. "Seriously?"

"I get the feeling she's not telling us everything."

"Such as?"

"Such as why Joe was at the office so late. According to

the police report, he didn't come home until eleven that night. And the break-in later that same night? Rebecca wasn't home at the time."

"I didn't know that," he said. "Was the little girl?"

"No. They were both away from the house. Convenient, huh?" he said.

"You expect her to be involved somehow? That would be tough."

"I hope not," Zack said fervently. "I came to help, but I'm not blind to who she is either."

"You don't think she's the murderer though, right?"

"No," he said, pausing. "Not the murderer. She isn't quite innocent either. She can be malicious. You just have to watch her interact with his own sister to see that."

"So it could have been a coincidence that she wasn't at home that night."

"Well, it sounds like we need to get some answers from her. I feel like Gemma has taken control of this, and we haven't even gotten in the front door of the investigation." Zack snorted. "Welcome to Gemma's world."

"Always taking charge?" Galen looked over where the two women stood on either side of the little girl, and a horse was up at the fence, her nose down so the little girl could pet her.

"No, not necessarily," Zack said. "I knew her ex though."

"She said he was ex-military."

"He turned mercenary once he was engaged to her. She didn't know about it."

"Ouch," he said. "I have a feeling she has very high morals, strong ethics, and wouldn't have approved. Especially if he didn't tell her. I doubt secrets fly with her either."

"Exactly," Zack said. "He, on the other hand, wanted more money, thinking he could provide better, and they could take off and have a better life. So, once he finished his time with the military, he used some of his connections to get private work in Africa. But, when she found out, she was in Switzerland. They had an almighty row, and he headed back and took a bullet from the person who should have been his target and died in the process."

"Ouch," Galen said. "So there's a bit of guilt on top of that."

"Guilt, anger, and a sense of betrayal, I imagine. All of it is rolled up inside."

"She's very controlled, and I don't think she says much or gives way to her feelings very often."

"And yet I would say Rebecca's the same. That's something they seem to have in common."

Chapter 6

THE REST OF the day passed in a series of outside adventure walks and a simple meal of ham sandwiches at lunch. After that, Gemma looked at Becky and said, "I'll go lie down again for a nap. How about you?"

Becky was already yawning and, with concurrence from Rebecca, the two groups split up.

As Gemma walked into her cabin, she threw herself down on the single bed, looked over at Galen, and said, "They'll bring another cot over for you."

"That would be good," he said, now seated on a lone chair in the room.

Picking up on the hesitation in his voice, she looked at him for a moment. "Look. I really am tired, and I do need to sleep, but it's obvious you have questions, so speak up." She curled up with a blanket over her shoulders, her eyes closed. She could feel him hesitating still, and she opened her eyes and said, "Or don't."

He gave a short bark of laughter. "You're very short and to the point."

"I don't suffer fools gladly," she murmured.

"Do you think your sister is involved in Joe's murder?"

"No." Clear and concise but nothing else was needed.

"Why was she not at home when Joe was murdered?"

"She was visiting a friend."

"Convenient," he replied.

"Yes."

"And her daughter? Where was she?"

"Becky was with her mother."

"Why was Joe working late? As in *late* late?"

She opened her eyes slowly and stared at him. "I don't know." And she wished she did. Staying an hour or two later was not his usual habit, she didn't think ...

"Did you not ask your sister?"

"I'm not sure I knew that he was working late that night," she said, staring across the cabin. "She said she wasn't home, and, when she got in the next morning, he was dead."

"So she found him?"

Gemma nodded slowly. "She was pretty traumatized when she called me."

"And did you believe her?"

"Yes," she said, remembering the pain in her sister's voice. The shock and horror of what had happened. Surely no one could fake that? "I did. My sister is a good actress, but that was real."

"Can you tell me where she found him?"

"In the hallway at the bottom of the stairs, still in his pajamas with a single gunshot to the head."

"Does that sound like a B&E gone wrong to you?"

"Of course not," she said. "He also had a handgun, but there was no sign of it when Rebecca went to give it to the police."

"So he came downstairs with a handgun potentially? And, if the intruder had a weapon, that would have upped the ante. He might have shot first in order to get away. A situation that built past what he'd expected."

"Potentially. I don't know."

Galen frowned. "I'd still like to locate Joe's gun."

"According to Rebecca, it's not in the house anymore."

"Do you know what kind of gun it was?"

Gemma shook her head. "Had no idea Joe had one at the house. With Becky around, I would have told him to toss the damn thing."

"Is it possible the robber wrestled it away from him and shot him with it?"

"Of course it's possible," she said. "But probable? I don't know."

"Joe was a big guy?"

"He was five feet, ten inches and about two-forty, with twenty pounds of paunch that he wore really well."

"Right," he said, studying her with an odd look in his eyes.

Then she should be used to that. Still, for some reason she wanted him to not be like everyone else. "Are you looking for a connection between my sister and Joe's death?"

"I just think it's highly irregular that she happened to be away and that the intruders would choose that night to come in."

"So, maybe the question is, who knew she wouldn't be there?"

"And who would that be?"

"Her girlfriend she stayed with," Gemma said instantly. "And her girlfriend's husband. He works with Joe too."

"And was he working that night?"

"Yes. The police investigated them and said they weren't suspects. I think the escalation at Joe's work is behind all this. Someone with a grudge. Were they just checking out his home, looking for something to steal, or did they go deliberately to kill him, I couldn't say."

"Okay," he said, "what else can you tell me about the crime scene? Like blood spatter. Did anybody look at it, or do we have any crime-scene photos? Do we have anything that connects Joe's death to Joe's predecessor at the brewery or the other thefts and break-ins at work?"

He watched the slight wince cross her face.

"I think they'd all have to be connected. Anything else is hard to contemplate. And I haven't seen any crime scene photos," she said faintly. "I can describe the scene as I saw it. He'd fallen forward, as if he were on the lower steps, took the bullet in his head, and stumbled to fall facedown at the bottom of the stairs. There was a huge blood pool around his head."

"Any around the back wall? The stairs?"

"Yes. I have no doubt that the spatter and the blood were all from the same shot."

"And he was in his pajamas?"

"Yes."

"Okay, so chances are that's how he was shot. What about fingerprints, the bullet, any casings, security cameras, keys to get in?"

"The back door was jimmied," she said, "although I'm not sure if it wasn't done afterward."

"You mean, to make it look like it was locked prior to entry?"

"Possibly. I don't know that. My mind just said something was off about the entire setup."

"More so than just a burglary?"

"I think it was all part of the same thing," she said. "I think somebody tried to make it look like a B&E, but the intention was to shoot Joe."

"Interesting. Who else would know that he was home

alone that night?"

"Whoever Rebecca might have told," she said. "I doubt Joe would have said anything."

"How was their marriage?"

"I thought it was fine, until hearing Rebecca bitch a little bit."

"Your sister bitches a lot." He asked, "So how can you tell when it's a little bit?"

"That's just who she is," she said with a half laugh. "She bitches about everything. I think it's part of her personality."

"It's exhausting," he said. "How do you do it?"

She nodded. "I'm used to it. But I'm not sure that was the persona she played with Joe. He loved her to distraction and just wanted the china doll to be his."

"And she was happy to be a china doll for him?" Galen asked.

"Absolutely. He bought her jewelry, nice clothes, and fancy stuff. He took her everywhere. She loved the life."

"*Hmm.* So then there's no reason for her to want to lose that, is there?"

"That's the biggest reason why I don't think she is really involved in this." At that, Gemma closed her eyes again.

"Unless she has a replacement in the wings?"

"I haven't heard of anybody."

"And yet my suggestion didn't shock you?"

She opened her eyes and stared at him. "I have no illusions about my sister," she said, "but even the bitches of the world have family, and she's part of mine."

"Good point," he said. "And yet you don't seem particularly close."

"I'd like to believe that underneath all the drama we are," she said, "but I can't be sure of it." She sighed, closing her eyes yet again.

"Any reason to suspect that Joe might have wanted a divorce?"

At that, her eyes popped open, and she stared at him in surprise.

He shrugged. "Just think about it. What if she would lose her marriage anyway? Do we know if there was any life insurance? A pension? She probably gets to keep the house, and she's the victim here and gets all the attention."

"That would be very low," she said. "Might be he had moved on, or wanted to, but I never saw or heard anything about that."

"But we don't know yet, do we?"

"Sounds to me," she said, "like you need to do some investigation on that."

He barked with laughter at that. "And here I thought that's what I was doing by talking to you."

"Let me know what you find when I wake up," she said, then rolled over to go to sleep.

"I'm not much help so far. What if I haven't found anything by then?" he asked curiously.

"Then you're not the man I think you are," she said and went silent.

GALEN STUDIED HER in amazement. Not only had she immediately dropped off to sleep, but she was so very unlike what he was used to. No, that wasn't quite true. He was used to this kind of temperament with the guys and gals he worked with but never with any women he met in the civilian world, for lack of a better term. Although he had worked with several who had similarities. Maybe that's why she was something odd, yet not so odd. He was confused by how to even label her. But as she slept here, her breathing slow and steady, he realized what it must have cost her to do this right now with him. It meant she had to trust him.

He got up slowly and walked to his laptop, grabbing it, meanwhile wondering if she was still just a little bit wary of him, yet extreme fatigue won out. She was seriously burned-out to drop off like that with him here. ... As he sat back down, her eye movements had slipped into one more level of unconsciousness, and he realized that she was in a deep sleep now. He turned on his laptop to see just what was going on. Galen sent messages to Levi, asking him for further information. He wanted crime-scene photos to match up with what he had just been told to confirm Gemma's recollection of it. He also wanted to know about life insurance and whether the couple had any recent marital problems.

Levi messaged back right away. **Isn't that something you should ask the wife?**

Galen replied, **I will when I have more intel. I wanted to hear what the general gossip has to say. Just in case their marital problems were not so secret.**

By the time Gemma woke up and slowly sat up, looking around in confusion, he had pretty well answered all the questions they had raised, confirming all that Gemma had said. The two society ladies Levi had spoken with confirmed that every marriage had problems and that Rebecca was a complainer anyway. Galen gently put down his laptop and quietly walked over, seeing a groggy and distant look in her gaze. He crouched in front of her. "Take it easy," he said. "You just woke up from a really deep sleep."

She nodded slowly. "It took me a moment to figure out where I was," she said, as she stifled a yawn. She looked around at the cabin. "I used to spend weeks of my summers here."

"And yet your sister didn't seem to know too much about this place."

"She never came with me," she said. "It was before our parents died, and it was my favorite place to come."

"Why is that?" he asked.

She smiled, slowly opening her eyes. "Because it took me back to nature and let me forget about the various levels of humanity that I struggled with."

"You must have been very happy here," he said.

"I was," she said, "but it also started changing around that time. I wasn't even sure if I should come back this time."

"Did they have all the weapons back then?"

She frowned and thought about it, then shook her head. "Not that I'm aware of, but that could be just because I was a teenager, and they didn't think I needed to know about them."

"That's possible too," he said. "They are very well weaponized now."

"The world isn't the same way it was ten years ago either," she countered.

"Do you have any reason to fear these people?"

"No," she said. "I've known Tim for a long time. But I don't want to bring any danger to him and his family and his friends. They have this life of peace, living off the land as much as they can and living on the fringe of society. All by choice. They know what society is like. They had an ugly situation a few years back that shifted the way they lived, as they were forced to protect themselves from another group."

"Are they aware of your situation?"

"Yes, and they opened the door to help me," she said. "However, I promised not to put anybody here in unnecessary danger."

"Well, let's hope you can honor that. As long as they understand it's still possible that the scenario could get ugly, then they will stay alert. Over the next couple days we'll see if anybody comes through Joe's cabin, who goes to Joe's house, and how much other information we can roust out. Maybe we can head back home after that."

She nodded slowly. "I know we can't disappear forever. I just wanted to step out of the world a little bit and cause everybody who was after my family to stop and rethink."

"Do you have any idea why they might want to take out Rebecca? Aside from the fact that she might have spoken to Joe of course."

"No," she said softly. "I've been racking my brain trying to think, but I'm not coming up with any answers that make sense."

"Maybe it's time to sit down and have a talk with Rebecca."

Chapter 7

GEMMA LOOKED AT Galen, gave him a sideways smile, and said, "Good luck with that."

"Will she even tell me?"

"I don't know if she will," she said. "It's not that she won't tell you. It's just that the answer isn't always clear."

"Yes or no isn't clear?"

"She ends up throwing a fit before you ever get the information you want from her."

"Well, that's usually a diversionary tactic."

"I know," she said softly, thinking about all the times her sister had gotten away from punishment and not having to fess up because of her tactics. "It doesn't mean that she's involved though. I often think it's just a game to her."

"It's hardly a game at this point though," he said quietly.

Just then a knock came on their cabin door.

"Who is it?" she asked, reaching up and yawning.

"Zack." He opened the door and stepped inside; Rebecca and Becky were right there beside him.

Becky raced over and launched herself into Gemma's arms. Gemma gave her a tight hug back. "I just woke up," Becky said.

"So did I," Gemma added.

And with that, Becky crawled up on the bed, pulling Gemma's blanket over her.

Gemma reached down and kissed the little girl on the cheek. "And here I thought you wanted to visit the rabbits."

Immediately Becky bolted from the bed. "Real rabbits? With long ears and fluffy tails?"

"Exactly," Gemma said with laughter. "Let me get my shoes on, and I'll take you over."

"How come you know about the rabbits?" Becky asked.

"Because I used to come here when I was growing up," she said. "We always had rabbits here."

"That must have been nice," Becky said and immediately turned to her mom. "How come I can't come here during my summers?"

"Why would you want to?" her mom asked, staring at her in distaste. "I mean, these animals poop everywhere."

Gemma stared at her in shock. "Is that the best you can come up with?"

"Whatever," she said. "I'm not looking at the rabbits."

"That's fine." Gemma walked over to the big pitcher of water on the counter and poured herself a glass. "We're expected at dinner in the long house tonight, by the way. I hope none of you have a problem with that."

"I have a headache," Rebecca said. "We still have plenty of food to make a sandwich. I'll just have that."

Gemma hesitated as she looked at her sister, realizing that the set look on her face was the same no matter what, and she nodded. "That would be fine." In fact, it would be preferable. Gemma didn't want to insult her host by having her sister be a petulant child at the dinner table. It would not be in anybody's best interest. She looked at the two men. "What about you two?"

They nodded and said they would be happy to join them at the long house.

She gave them both a quiet smile. "Good," she said. "I'll make that arrangement while I'm out with Becky. I'll find out what time we're expected for dinner too." She held out her hand to Becky. "Come on. Let's go see the rabbits."

Immediately the little girl raced over and chattered about what colors and how many there were.

Gemma turned, looked at the men, nodded toward her sister, and said, "This might be a good time." She walked out, heading across to the rabbit hutches, leaving the cabin behind.

Becky asked Gemma, "A good time for what?"

"To ask your mom some questions."

"She doesn't like questions," Becky said. "They make her feel terrible."

"I don't know if it's the questions that make her feel terrible," Gemma said, "but I imagine trying to find the answers might."

"Yes," she said, "I hate having questions when I don't know the answers."

"Especially in school," Gemma said, laughing.

At that, her niece wrinkled up her face. "I can get most of those questions," she said. "It's all those other questions," she said, with a big eye roll as she danced at her aunt's side.

"And who are asking those other questions?" she asked.

"Daddy's friends."

Her niece answered so innocently, and yet Gemma was shocked by the answer. "When did you talk to Daddy's friends?"

"Since Daddy died." She stopped for a moment and asked, "Is Daddy in heaven?"

"Absolutely he is," Gemma said instantly. "You know he wouldn't have left you for anything, right?"

"I know," Becky said sadly. "He loved me."

"And he wanted to be here for you," Gemma added, "but sometimes we don't get what we want." Gemma remembered hearing Joe say that many a time. "And your daddy would have told you that over and over again, wouldn't he? But he also always would have told you that we still have to keep trying to do what's right."

"I'll be a doctor," Becky said. "Then I can save people like my daddy."

"And that would be lovely, if that's what you end up doing," she said, smiling down at her niece. "We need more doctors."

She nodded, and the two of them headed across the field. Gemma was trying to figure out what questions had been asked of her niece and who had asked her. But it was a matter of making the questions about that appear subtle and innocent.

"What kind of questions couldn't you answer when they asked you? When I was in class," she said, "they used to ask me questions about history, and I never could answer those."

"I don't know much history," she said. "They asked me about Mommy."

"Oh, interesting. But then your mother is very beautiful, so, of course, they asked questions about her."

"And about Daddy."

"Like what?" she asked as she led Becky over to the hutch.

"They asked if Mommy and Daddy were really close and if they talked. And if Daddy might have shown her something."

"Something like what?"

The little girl shrugged. "They talked about some ladder

or something." She frowned. "I don't know. That isn't quite the right word."

"Ledger?"

Immediately Becky nodded. "That's it. What is that?"

"It's a book where people record stuff."

"Yeah, they asked if there was a book."

"That your Daddy might have had?"

She nodded.

"What did you tell him?"

"Well, Daddy had a book," she said, "but I don't know where it is now."

"When did you last see it?"

"Mommy had it," she said, delivering a bombshell that Gemma hadn't even considered.

"WHAT WAS THAT last line of Gemma's? About 'this might be a good time?' What the hell does that mean?" Rebecca asked, as she walked over to a small table. "I prefer my cabin. It's nicer."

"That's because it's bigger, has a bedroom, and more furniture," Zack said patiently.

"But then there's more of us over there, so that makes sense to be there," Rebecca said. She looked at the two men. "Why are you catering to Gemma? You know we don't have to be here."

"Don't we?" Galen asked. "I have a bunch of questions to ask you."

"I hate questions," she said. "The police interviewed me for hours. It was terrible."

"But they were only doing what they needed to do," Galen said. "Finding out what happened to your husband. They have procedures to follow."

"Sure," she said, bored. "Ask away then."

"What was your relationship like with Joe?"

She stopped, looked up at him, and frowned. "We were happy. Why? Has somebody said anything?"

"No," he said, "we just need to know."

"No," she snapped, glaring at him. "You don't need to know."

Zack sighed and looked out the window.

Galen hid a smile. "Are you always this difficult?" She turned on him, and he could see her fury building. "I won't be sidetracked, you know?" he said mildly. "We have other questions. Were you two talking about divorce at all?"

"No," she snapped. "We were happy."

"Was there life insurance on Joe?"

"Yes."

"Have you received a payout?"

"Not yet."

"How much?"

"Half a million," she replied.

At that, Zack whistled. "That should set you up nicely."

"I hope so," she said, with a shrug of her shoulders, "but it won't be quite enough, and you know it."

"Quite enough for what?" Galen asked.

"To rebuild my life," she said. "Joe was everything to me."

"And yet you never talk about missing him. Even the money isn't enough to rebuild your life, but you don't talk about rebuilding that empty piece of your heart."

"I loved him as much as I've loved anyone," she said, boldly staring at him. "I know most people don't think I have feelings. I'm not superficial as much as I just don't know what deep feelings are. Maybe something is wrong with me, but I don't care. It's who I am, and people just need to accept it."

"Did you have anything to do with Joe's death?"

"Of course not," she said. "That's insulting."

"That's a lot of insurance money too," he said mildly.

She just glared at him.

"Do you have any idea why Joe was killed?" he continued.

"Gemma thinks it has to do with his work."

"I'm not asking what Gemma thinks," he said, again seeing her tactics to evade the questions.

She glared at him. "No, I don't know. It was a robbery gone wrong. To think it was anything else is just trying to stir up trouble."

"Did you ever see Joe hide any material? Did you ever see any work he brought home? Or did he have any suspicious information on somebody? Any reason he would get blackmailed?"

"No, I don't think so," she said. "I have no idea though."

"What do you mean, you have no idea?" He studied her like the odd specimen she was. Was the sister lying? He voted for the sister lying. She hadn't spoken much about her husband, and the words that had come out of her mouth weren't anything he could believe.

"I have no idea," she said, raising her hands in frustration. "He probably just got hold of some information and was killed for it. At least that's a possibility. He said he'd found something at work but didn't say what it was." She looked like she was considering the idea, then shrugged as if she didn't care. "I didn't have anything to do with his work.

I didn't care to know anything. So don't ask me any more questions as I don't have any answers."

"Maybe you do, and maybe you don't," he said.

"Well, that's for somebody else to figure out," she said. "I don't know."

He nodded. "So you've never seen anything? You didn't see him talking to anybody in an animated way or some stranger you didn't recognize? Nobody ever put pressure on him or on you? He never told you that he was being black-mailed or that what he was doing was dangerous? Nothing like that?"

She shrugged. "No."

"Had Joe changed in any way in the last few months?"

"He was more secretive, yes. I wondered if he was having an affair, but, when I asked him, he laughed and denied it."

"And you believed him?"

"Sure," she said. "He's never lied to me before."

"And yet, when I asked you if there were any problems between the two of you and your marriage, you said no."

"Because it was a no," she said. "He told me nothing was going on, and I believed him. That means there was no problem in our marriage."

"Right," he said. "And what about the guy who was breaking into your house?"

"He probably heard that I was there alone, and figured I was an easy mark, and he could get in and get out with a few items."

"And where were you the night Joe died?"

"I was at my friend Melanie's house," she said. "And Becky was with me. No, I didn't set it up ahead of time. No, I didn't know Joe would get killed. And, no, I have no clue as to who might have killed him."

"Well, it was a breaking and entering, right?"

"Exactly," she said. "So it could have been anyone." She flounced over to the doorway. "Those are the same questions the cops asked me. And I still don't have any different answers."

"That's a good thing," he said calmly. "You're not supposed to have different answers."

She looked momentarily confused and then glared at him. "If that's a trick question or something, I don't appreciate it. I didn't have anything to do with Joe's death."

"And yet you don't seem too broken up over it."

"He loved me," she said, her voice quiet. "For that, I will always miss him. Did I love him? I really don't know. But it was comfortable, and I was happy." And, with that, she turned and walked out.

Zack walked out behind her without saying a word but not before giving Galen an eye roll at Rebecca's answers.

Galen sat in the living room of the small single-room cabin and thought about a woman who was honest enough to say that her husband adored her and looked after her and that she would miss that part but not necessarily him. It's too bad Galen didn't have a chance to ask Joe these questions. Maybe Joe wasn't all that happy. Maybe Joe was looking to change things, and maybe Rebecca just didn't know.

Chapter 8

G EMMA STOPPED AT the long house and stepped in to say hello to Tim. He looked up and smiled. When he saw Becky, he grinned and said, "I saw you over by the rabbits."

She beamed. "There are baby rabbits," she said.

"That there is. We've got five babies right now." He looked up at Gemma. "Is everybody coming for dinner?"

"Three adults, one child," she said with a smile. "Becky's mother has a bad headache, so she'll likely be down for the day."

"Oh, dear," he said with a frown. "Do you think she'd like a bowl of soup and maybe some fresh buns to go with it?"

"You know what? She might," Gemma said with a smile. "She tends to prefer to lie in the quiet. Then, when she feels better, she'll want to eat."

"Exactly," he said. "When you go home from dinner, we can send you with a bowl."

"Thank you," she said. "I just came to check in. What time is dinner?"

"How is five-thirty?"

"That would be lovely." Turning, she held out her hand for Becky, and the two of them walked back outside again. She stopped on the huge veranda, wondering at how oddly not-at-home she felt here this time. In her teens, she had come year after year, cheering the people on, the lifestyle, the break away from her family.

"Did you really like spending time here?" Becky asked her aunt.

"I did," she said, "but, like everything in life, things change."

"Good," she said. "I'm glad you did. I like being here too. Is it the same people?"

"Not all of them, no," she said. "Only a few of them are still the same."

Maybe that was the reason. Everybody else seemed more like brothers and sisters to her back then, but a long enough time had passed, and she was now an outsider. It was still the right place to come because nobody would find her here, but, at the same time, it wasn't the same as what it had been. And maybe that was normal too. Maybe life kept moving on, and she was supposed to move on with it.

Although that would have to wait until this mess was over. She knew Galen wasn't a fan of her sister, and most of the time Gemma wasn't either. But she loved her. They could never be best friends because they were too different, but family was family. And they both loved Becky.

Gemma had no doubt about that. And, for that, she could forgive her sister for a lot. But then according to Becky there was a lot going on here that Gemma didn't know. She needed to tell Galen about what Becky had said about the ledger too. Not knowing when there'd be a right time, she quickly sent him a text.

While she waited for a response, she realized how being here again had brought up a plethora of emotions she'd hoped she'd dealt with a long time ago. Tim had taken on a role of father, family friend, confident, and therapist. Helping her deal with the lack of love in her life and the excess of narcissism.

She'd blossomed here. Had learned self-control here. More important, she'd learned self-confidence. And, for that, she owed Tim everything.

She couldn't imagine her life if she hadn't had this place to escape to summer after summer. She'd have been left alone and likely would have become very introverted. Tim had saved her. Helped raised her. And, indeed, had become the person she'd emulated on her way to adulthood. She'd never forgive herself if she brought hardship down on his shoulders now.

Her phone buzzed. One word answer from Galen.

Bitch.

She smiled at that.

"I'm hungry," Becky announced suddenly. She sniffed the air around them. "What's that smell?"

"Fresh air," Gemma said drily. "I know it's not something you're used to." She bent down and picked up a purple wildflower for the little girl. "See these? I used to pick bouquets of these for the dinner table every day."

"Can we tonight?" Becky asked excitedly, dancing around and clapping her hands.

"Sure. Why not?" And she laughed as Becky raced around, collecting a mix of colorful varieties to take indoors. As soon as she had picked what she could find close by, she turned to Gemma. "Is this enough?"

"Yes, I think so. Let's go find Tim and give it to him."

And that's what they did, running through the long grass. Showing Becky what Gemma's summers had been like took Gemma back to her childhood. By the time they made it to the long house, they were both out of breath and sporting rosy cheeks.

Tim stood on the long covered veranda, grinning at them. "Aren't you two a pretty picture," he said in that calm voice of his.

Gemma likened it the guiding light in her world, and she'd love for Becky to spend time with him.

"This is for the dinner table," Becky said, proudly holding out her bouquet.

"Mighty fine flowers those are," he said with a nod. "And brings back a lot of lovely memories. Come on inside. I'm sure Gemma remembers where the vases are for those."

The three walked inside to see the rest of the clan busily setting the table for dinner. Their loud exclamations over the flowers made Becky's grin widen and her eyes sparkle.

And made Gemma's heart sigh with happiness.

GALEN WALKED INTO the long house to see the rest of his group standing off to one side, speaking with several people. He joined them and casually slid a hand onto Gemma's shoulder. She turned in surprise, then smiled at him, and stepped back slightly to include him in the group. He appreciated that. Everything about her appeared to be very honest, but anything beyond what she wanted you to see was very hard to read.

Just then a big bell rang. She chuckled. "Is that still the same bell?"

Tim nodded. "It works. Why fix it?"

At her urging, Galen took a spot beside her at the table, with little Becky on the other side. The huge table must have easily seated thirty-five to forty people. He was amazed at the length of it.

Gemma smiled at Tim. "This table holds a lot of good memories for me," she said easily.

Tim nodded. "You spent a lot of summers here. It's great to see you again."

His voice held such warmth and naturalness that she relaxed a little more. She'd come, if just to reconnect.

As they talked, large platters of food were placed at various positions on the table, and Galen noted three of everything, so each group of twelve people or so could work off the same three platters. One was full of massive vegetables, another full of roasted potatoes, and another with roasted chickens cut up. Then bowls of salad appeared. He was amazed at the amount of food here, but he dug in quite hardily.

He stayed quiet as he listened to the talk going on around him. Zack was on the other side of Becky, carrying on a conversation with somebody at Tim's side, both who were across from Gemma. Galen really appreciated the simplicity of the area. And the food. The vegetables here were … tastier. He was studying a carrot when Tim spoke up.

"They're from our own gardens."

"I presume that's why they taste so good," he murmured before taking a bite. They held so much flavor.

Tim relaxed and nodded. "That's exactly why they taste so good."

Galen finished his meal a little bit fast because he'd really enjoyed it and had been hungry, and, when Tim nudged some of the leftover food on the platters his way, he took seconds of the vegetables. When he was done, he said to Tim with a smile, "Compliments to the chef. That was truly excellent."

Tim nodded his head. "Everyone here does an incredible job."

Galen sat back and relaxed, looking at Becky as she pushed a carrot around her plate. He smiled at the little girl as Gemma looked on. "You know, Becky, I'm sure if you asked, they'd show you where they actually grow those."

Becky looked at the carrot and then back at Galen. "They grow?"

Galen chuckled. "They grow in the ground. They probably have a big garden here with lots of carrots and other things too."

"Can I see them?" she demanded of Tim.

"Sure you can," Tim said, nodding slowly, "but we don't waste food here."

Instantly the piece of carrot popped into Becky's mouth, and she chewed it. "I like raw carrots," she said, "but I don't really like cooked ones."

"But how is that cooked one?" Tim asked with a chuckle.

"It's good," she said in surprise. "Much better than the ones Mom cooks."

At that, everybody had a good laugh.

When dinner was done, coffee was brought out with dessert. Although Galen was full, he wasn't stuffed. It gave him a deeper understanding of how this place worked when several young women collected all the dishes and then brought out pound cake all sliced up, with several urns of coffee.

Becky crowed in delight. "There's cake, Aunt Gemma. There's cake."

"There is, indeed," she said. "And one of my favorites. I

spent many an evening making pound cake here," she said laughing. "We made dozens at a time."

"And as I remember," Tim said, with a paternal smile on his face, "you got to be a right good hand at it."

"Hard to mess it up." She took a slice, broke off a little piece, and popped it in her mouth. With a happy sigh she said, "It tastes like memories."

And wasn't that an interesting statement. Galen broke off a piece and popped it into his mouth. "I don't know about the memories part," he said, "but it's really good."

Gemma smiled at him.

When the conversation wound down, and the rest of the dishes were cleaned away, Galen got to his feet, looked over at Becky. "How about a walk to take a look at the garden where you can see the carrots grow?"

"Yes!" She pushed back her chair and started to leave, then stopped, came back to look at Tim, and said, "Thank you very much for my dinner."

A pleased smile broke across his face, and he tilted his head in her direction. "You are most welcome."

Galen looked down at Gemma. "You want to come?"

She smiled at him. "Sure." She stood, and he held out his hand, surprised when, quite naturally, she took it.

Hand in hand, the two of them walked out with Becky racing ahead.

As they got outside, Gemma asked quietly, "Were you trying to keep me away from them?"

"No, not at all," he said. "I just thought Becky might feel more comfortable if you were with us."

"She probably would be," Gemma said, "but she's taken to you quite naturally."

"You told her that I was a friend of yours," he said, "and

that gave her a stamp of approval."

"I was hoping it would."

"You know Tim quite well?"

"I've known Tim for decades," she said.

"You obviously didn't have too grand of a childhood if you found your love and acceptance here among strangers."

"No," she said. "It wasn't a good childhood at all. For my sister it was. She was the chosen one, the beautiful child, and the perfect little baby. I was the solemn, quiet, and slightly gawky older child, who did everything that she was told but never with the same grace or beauty as my sister."

No rancor was in her voice. No criticism, disappointment, or resentment. He appreciated that. "And, then again, you were also a simpler child. You preferred a garden of fresh vegetables to the latest makeup, pretty toy, or seeing the newest shopping center. I presume your mother was more high-maintenance, like Rebecca?"

"And my father," she said with a smile. "They were both clotheshorses and were all about appearances. They wouldn't have wanted to touch the ground with their fingers, no way, no how."

"I'm surprised they even let you come here."

"Don't be," she said. "I begged to come the first time, and, after that, I wouldn't leave them alone because I just kept wanting to come back."

"Do you think they ever did any kind of research into this place to make sure you were safe?"

She tilted her head to the side as they walked. "I don't know," she said. "The first time I came for three weeks. The second time I came for six. Then, after that, I came for the whole summer holiday."

"That would have built a divide between you and your

sister."

"Yes. She hated the very idea of this place, didn't see the draw to me, but the divide was already there, so it didn't need a whole lot of building."

"Yet you still look after her."

"She's still my sister," she said. "It doesn't really matter how one looks at it. Blood is blood."

"As long as some reciprocity exists in the relationship."

"I'm not sure about that," she said. "I suffer no illusions where my sister is concerned. I don't want to say that she's shallow, but I know that's how she appears."

"She absolutely appears that way," he said with a laugh. "It's hard to see her in any other light. And, if you doubt it, just wait until she opens her mouth."

"And I'm not sure that's fair," she said. "My parents were similar in many ways."

"That surprises me," he said.

"Why? People like her grow up to be adults too," she said with a smile. "Then they find others who are the same way, and they marry, start another generation with the same issues."

"Good point," he said. "Was Joe like that?"

She shook her head. "No. Not at all. Joe was very special. He was a good man."

"And maybe deserved more than her?"

"You'd have pissed him right off if you'd said something like that to him," she said, laughing. "He was head over heels in love with her. He knew who she was, what she was, and he loved her in spite of it."

"Good for him. And even luckier for her," he said.

"Exactly," she replied with a smile.

They walked up to a large fenced area. Becky stared in

from the outside. "What is all this?" she cried out.

From what he could see, it was a massive garden, several hundred feet long and wide. "This is a really big garden," he murmured.

"A lot of people are here now," Gemma said, "but it wasn't this big when I was here originally. It's definitely grown. A lot." She opened the gate and let Becky in. Slowly they wandered up and down the aisles, where she could see everything growing, from beets and radishes to lettuce, carrots, potatoes, and even peanuts.

The back section had nut trees and fruit trees. When Becky saw the first recognizable vegetable she was enthralled. She asked a dozen questions, and Galen had to admit he was happy to see the innocence of her young mind as she caught on to where her food came from. She danced and clapped her hands with joy, even as the sun started to set. She looked over at the beautiful sunset and gave a happy sigh. "This is a beautiful place, Auntie Gemma."

"It is. Now you know why I came here so often."

"Why don't you still come?" she asked. "I could come with you."

She chuckled. "Who knows? But it is definitely time for bed."

"Really? It's too early. It's time to go back maybe, but not to bed."

"Well, I guess it depends on how tired you are," she said. "Let's head to the cabins before we can't see the path in front of us. It gets really dark at night here."

Galen noted Zack standing outside their cabin, and, as he saw them, he walked down the stairs to join them.

"How is my sister?" Gemma asked.

Zack shrugged. "I haven't been back to her cabin yet."

Gemma nodded and turned in the direction of their two cabins. "We should check in and make sure she doesn't want that soup that Tim offered earlier and that I forgot to mention as I walked out."

"Well then, we'll ask her and come back if she does," he said. As they headed down the pathway to the two nearby cabins, yet farther away from the rest of the group, Zack asked, "So how were the gardens?"

Becky bounced with all the answers about how wonderful it was.

He chuckled. "Glad to see you enjoyed it," he said. "What will you do now? Bug your mom for a garden at home?"

"I wish," she said, "but you know she'll say no."

Surprised at the answer and the wisdom behind it, Gemma turned to look at her niece. "Maybe she would let you have a pot at least. You could plant all kinds of things in a big pot."

"Maybe," she said, "but I figure that I might get bored with it real fast."

"Will you?" Galen asked.

"I don't know," she said. "I do that now sometimes."

"Maybe that's just because you haven't found anything that really interests you yet," Galen said in surprise at her unusual maturity. As if bits of Gemma were showing up in her personality. He hoped so for the child's sake.

"Maybe."

As they headed to the cabin, Gemma called out, "Rebecca, how are you doing?"

No answer.

Zack jumped ahead of them and opened the door. "Rebecca?"

No answer. They immediately raced inside and spread out through the small cabin.

"She couldn't have gone far," Gemma said, looking at the others.

Galen shook his head and pointed out in the back, where they'd parked. Only Zack's vehicle was there. Gemma's was missing.

Chapter 9

G EMMA STARED AT the empty space in shock. "She wouldn't have left without us, would she?"

"I don't know her anymore," Zack said quietly. "She wasn't very happy about being here."

"No," she said, "but surely no way she'd leave Becky behind." That wasn't the sister she knew. No, she'd have grabbed Becky, then buggered off without a care for anyone else.

"She left her with you, so that's a different story," Galen said.

Gemma shrugged. "I think that's splitting hairs."

"I'll go check the laptops," he said.

She looked at him with sudden understanding and nodded. "Good idea. Becky, let's go see if your mom left a note, saying where she might have gone," Gemma said. "Where do you think she would have hidden it?"

Immediately Becky headed to her bed. "There's nothing on her pillow."

"*Great,*" Gemma said as she searched every other surface. Inside, her heart slammed against her chest. "Are we thinking this is bad?" she murmured to Zack.

He looked at her steadily. "It's not good."

"After all the efforts we've gone through to keep her safe, I don't understand why she would do this."

"The trouble is," he said, "do we know whether she's actually done it or if somebody did it to her."

Gemma winced at that. "I was trying to avoid that, which is pretty rough if that is the case. Would they have taken just her and not Becky?" she whispered.

"If they couldn't get a hold of Becky, maybe," he said.

Just then her phone rang. "Hello?"

"It's me," Rebecca said in a hoarse whisper. "Oh, God, you've got to come. I've been kidnapped."

"What are you talking about?" she said. "You drove out of here in my car."

"Yes, I did," she said. "I just went back to Joe's cabin though. I thought I could pick up a few things to make it a little easier. You know how little bedding there is at that hippie commune."

"That's hardly the point now," Gemma said, rubbing her temple. "Where are you exactly?"

"I'm in the cabin," she snapped, "but people are here."

"You said you were kidnapped."

"Well, I haven't been yet," she said waspishly, "but men are downstairs. It's not like they are going to let me leave. You have to come and get me out of here."

"Yes, we're on the way," she said. "You need to hide and stay hidden." At that, the phone went dead. She turned to look right at Zack, who was already racing to the door. "Why would she do that?" she muttered.

"It doesn't matter," Zack said. "You stay here with Becky."

She stared at him and frowned.

Galen returned and told them, "I just checked the laptop, and the cameras picked up people at Joe's cabin. Rebecca too."

She held up her phone. "My sister just called me. First, she told me that she was kidnapped, then changed it, saying she was hiding upstairs and people were down below. She wants us to go get her."

Galen looked at her, startled. "You stay here with Becky, and we'll be back in a bit." He and Zack bolted out the front door.

Becky grabbed Gemma's hand. "Is Mommy okay?

"She is at the moment," she answered, "but she went back to the other cabin."

"Why?" Becky cried out. "It's nice here."

"I don't know, honey. Your mom has a mind of her own."

"She didn't want to leave our house. She said it was her home. And Joe left it to her. She's mad at you for bringing her here. I'm not. I like it here."

"Good. I don't know if your daddy left it to her or not." She turned to look at Becky. "Why did you call your daddy Joe?"

"That's what Mommy said to call him. But he was my daddy, wasn't he?"

She nodded slowly. "Yes."

Becky sighed. "Sometimes I wondered."

"Wondered if he was?"

"Yes. Mommy told Daddy that I wasn't his."

"Ouch," she said, staring at the little girl with sad fascination. "That must have been rough."

"Daddy was upset," she said pragmatically.

"I'd be terribly upset if somebody told me that you weren't mine," Gemma said, reaching out an arm and hugging the little girl. "I think your mom was angry, and that's why she said it. People say all kinds of things they don't mean when they're angry, honey." She closed the front door and motioned to the couch. "Want me to put on some hot chocolate?"

Immediately Becky smiled. "Yes, please! Thank you."

A chill had settled in the room now that the sun had set. Their cabin had a wood-burning fireplace, but she hadn't looked for any logs. It was summertime, but it still would have been comforting to have a fire. She walked over to the little two-burner gas stove and heated up some water. She was pretty sure hot chocolate mix would be in the cabin. If not this one, at least in hers. When she couldn't find any, she turned off the water.

"Let's go to my cabin. I think the hot chocolate is over there." Becky immediately hopped up, and, holding hands, they walked over to Gemma's little cabin. As they neared hers, she caught movement of someone or something behind the cabins. Frowning, she looked down at Becky. "*Shh*, let's play quiet."

Becky looked up but seemed to have some understanding that something was wrong, and she nodded.

Together the two tiptoed inside the cabin, while Gemma watched as much as she could from the back window. With no lights on in this cabin, and the lights still on in the other one, she could see a single male approaching from the back. She didn't recognize his shape. It definitely wasn't Zack or Galen, and neither was it Tim. Hating this, she immediately packed up the little bit of clothing and things that they had. "We have to be really, really quiet."

"Are we leaving again?"

"We might be, yes."

As the stranger circled around Rebecca's empty cabin, he disappeared in the front door. She knew that very quickly he'd be coming to see if they were here. She grabbed up her bag, realizing that Galen's bag was here, but not much else was left. He must have taken his laptop and some of his gear. She quickly packed all that was here, but she couldn't carry it all. She held out her hand, dropped everything, and took the little girl and headed over toward the long house. It was a well-worn path, and they could walk quietly.

When they got up to the main cabin, Tim stood outside, smoking a cigarette. "Did you need something?"

"Somebody's walking around our cabins. It's not one of us," she said in a low tone.

His gaze sharpened. "Well, shouldn't be anybody over there at all," he said.

"I watched him circle my sister's cabin, and then he went inside."

"And who was in there?" he asked. He looked down at the two of them. "Where's her mother?"

She quickly explained. Tim shook his head. "You know that some people you can't ever help."

"I know," she said. "I keep trying to get her out of trouble, but—"

"I'll take a look." He stopped, gazed at the little girl, and said, "I'll have to take a gun. Will that bother you?"

She shook her head, but her bottom lip trembled.

Gemma gripped Becky's hand firmly. "We'll be fine," she said to Becky with a confident smile she wasn't feeling. "Won't we?"

Becky squeezed her hand and nodded.

"Good," Tim said. "Let's go check it out."

"We'll probably be too late by now," she said.

"Maybe so, but it's better to check it out while we can."

"Got it," she said, and, resolutely, with Becky at her side, she turned and followed Tim back the way they came.

GALEN AND ZACK parked off the road in the brush. Silently the two men got out and slipped through the trees toward Joe's cabin. It was nearly dark, and they blended in well. They stayed within ten feet of each other until they approached the cabin; then one went to the left, the other to the right.

Galen himself came up around the back and approached the kitchen. In his mind he remembered the layout. No spare vehicle was here, and that bothered him. If at least two guys were involved, and Galen knew there was because he had seen them on the security footage, where were they now?

He slipped into the kitchen. No lights were on, so he stopped and listened intently, searching for sounds of breathing, sounds of somebody having noticed that they'd arrived. But he heard no sounds of anybody. He moved through the kitchen, dining room, living room, and came face-to-face with Zack, his face dark and angry as he shook his head. They raced up the stairs, checking to see if anybody was there. When they didn't find anything, he called out lightly, "Rebecca, are you here?"

Silence.

"Shit," Galen heard Zack whisper beside him.

That was exactly how Galen felt. Because it meant that they'd missed them. It hadn't been more than ten minutes, maybe fifteen now, since the phone call. So Rebecca may have been heard and had been grabbed and taken. But then, who the hell knew where they were now?

Galen and Zack had come down the highway without lights on and hadn't seen another vehicle going either way.

For a stretch of about one-quarter mile, they would have seen somebody leave. So, chances were that she'd been found, immediately snatched, and taken out of here. But so fast after her call to Gemma?

Galen had his laptop with him, but he couldn't get a good internet connection at first. He walked around until he got better reception. So the kidnappers had taken her out through the kitchen and then the front door of Joe's cabin. After another quick pass through the security tapes, he pulled out his phone and called Gemma. When she answered in a low tone, he immediately knew there was trouble. "What's the matter?"

"Somebody just entered and searched Rebecca's cabin," she said. "I'm here with Tim, but I see no sign of anyone now. We just came back to search. I'd taken Becky over to the main building, and Tim came back with us. But whoever it was is gone now."

"And so is Rebecca," he said. "We're at Joe's cabin, but there's no sign of her. No sign of anybody."

"What about the video feed?" she asked.

"I've got my laptop here, but it's not connecting well."

"I'm walking back over to see what I can find out on mine," she said.

He listened as she sat down to check it out.

"I just backed it up fifteen minutes. Give me a second."

A period of silence was followed by a long sigh.

"They've got her," she spoke in a soft voice. "I can see her being walked out the front door."

"Are they holding a weapon on her?" he asked.

"I can't tell," she answered. "It's only showing the heads. And I can only see the back of hers."

"What about the camera outside? Can you see a vehicle?"

"It's a small pickup," she said, "similar to yours."

"It's not ours though," he said. "Ours is hid in the brush."

"This was off to the side, and I could just barely see the outline."

"Okay," he said. "We're coming back to get you."

"No," she said. "Becky and I are safe here with Tim. Go after Rebecca. Please."

He hesitated. The note of desperation in her voice got to him. "We'll do a check," he said, "but it depends on how far ahead they are."

"It can't be more than ten minutes," she said. "You know you can overtake them if that's the case."

"Yes," he said, "I can, but I don't really like leaving you back there."

"Don't worry about me," she said. "Becky and I are here, and we're fine. Nobody here will hurt us."

"Maybe," he said. "But you have to remember, you can't trust everybody there just because you knew some of them a long time ago."

"I know," she said. "I've been reassessing a lot of my choices right now. But please, you're closest, so go after Rebecca." And, with that, she hung up.

Galen turned to look back at Zack. "She wants us to go after Rebecca."

"Of course she does," he said, as he tapped his laptop screen, staring at it. "They're not that far ahead of us."

"They are about fifteen minutes ahead, I'd say," Galen stated. By now they were already inside the vehicle, with Zack driving, Galen taking over Zack's laptop. "I still don't understand the why of this though."

"I'm not sure either," Zack said. "I noticed you asked if

they had weapons."

"A part of me doesn't trust Rebecca," he said. "A part that still wonders if she was involved in Joe's death somehow. I'm worried that Rebecca is not as sweet, innocent, and useless as she tries to appear."

Zack shot him a hard look. "I hope you're wrong for that little girl's sake."

"I hope I am too," he said, but inside he didn't think he was. "Just drive, and we'll get to the bottom of this eventually."

"But Joe's already dead," Zack said. "We've got to make sure there aren't any others."

"No," Galen said. "We've got to make sure that if anyone else dies, it's not us. But I'm totally okay taking out the asshole who killed a good family man for trying to do the right thing."

Chapter 10

GEMMA STAYED AT the long house where they'd had dinner, as Tim spoke with several other people. He'd organized a search of the entire ten-acre property. Groups of men had headed out, and the women were checking all the log buildings.

Gemma looked at him. "I didn't think anybody would have come here, would have even known to come here. And we weren't followed. I found no tracker on my car or my things."

"It's standard procedure to track via satellite, even for the bad guys," he said easily. "Times have changed since you were here—and not in a good way."

She raised an eyebrow.

He smiled. "Not us. I mean in the world."

"I hear you," she said with a nod. "I thought the world was headed to a much better place, but it seems like it's going downhill rapidly."

"Only if you let that attitude into your consciousness," he said, reaching out to tap her head.

She laughed. "You were always really good with that kind of stuff."

"And so were you. What happened?"

"I got busy in the world," she said. "And of course my ex-fiancé changed my viewpoint a bit."

"Yes," he said. "Things like that would do it." He smiled. "Remember though, there's always light. You chose darkness. The other is out there any time you want to reach for it."

She smiled. He had always had a very simplistic way of looking at the world. She appreciated it, yet, at the same time, knew it was an easy way to look at life from here. Especially because, living the way Tim and the others did, he got to stay away from the incessant ugly news, murders, and terrible wars going on around the world. Because of the work she did, she traveled globally, and it kept her very much up on a lot of what was going on out there. She preferred his world but was mired in hers. At least for now.

She rubbed her arms, wishing she was with Galen and Zack. Becky sat beside her, coloring with several other little girls.

She looked up at Gemma. "Mom'll be okay, right?"

She smiled. "Of course. Your mom is always okay."

Becky nodded solemnly and went back to her coloring. Gemma sighed.

The truth was, Rebecca always seemed to land on her feet somehow. Gemma just hoped that this whole scenario would turn out better than she thought it might. Her sister wasn't so much selfish as self-centered. If Rebecca thought she would lose the cushy lifestyle she had right now, she might have done something to change the status quo.

As Gemma sat here, her hands cradling a cup of tea, several of the men came back and shook their heads at Tim. He smiled and nodded. "In this case, no news is good news," he said.

Several women, who had been waiting in the main cabin, got up with the men, and they all left.

"I gather they found nothing," Gemma said.

He smiled and nodded. "Nothing that they shouldn't have found."

Gemma looked over at Becky. "What about you? Are you ready to head back to the cabin?"

Becky shrugged her shoulders. She didn't seem to be too bothered about her mother, and Gemma wanted to keep it that way. At least for a little bit longer. Anything she could do to make it easier for the little girl was better.

Finally her niece looked up, put down her crayons, and came around to the table where Gemma sat. She wrapped her arms around her waist and tucked up close.

"Everything will be okay, sweetheart."

Becky rubbed her head against Gemma's chest in a facsimile of a nod and squeezed tighter.

"Tim, we'll head back over," Gemma said with a smile. "Stay in for the night."

He nodded. "Do you want a light to get you over there?"

"We'll be fine," she assured him.

"The fireplace works too," he said, "and we had the chimney cleaned not too long ago."

She smiled in delight. "In that case, how about marshmallows?" she asked Becky.

The little girl lifted her head, and stars lit up her gaze. "Over the fire?"

"Sure. Why not?" she said.

Just then, Tim returned with a small bag of marshmallows and a couple sticks. She laughed. With the sticks and marshmallows in one hand, her niece's hand in the other, they headed back toward the cabin. The least Gemma could do was make this as much fun as possible for Becky's sake. If bad news was coming, the two of them could do nothing to change it. But at least this would make a happy memory to go with it.

"A VEHICLE'S UP ahead of us," Zack said. "I caught a glimpse of it."

They drove without lights, grateful that the moon gave them enough light to see the road in front of them. It was a backwoods highway with no traffic, and so far they hadn't met anybody coming or going. But up ahead they could see taillights now, and the halo glow in front of a vehicle.

"Good thing," Galen said. "We've been driving for half an hour at well past top speed."

"Who knew the old girl had it in her?" Zack said, patting the steering wheel lightly.

"It's got to be them," Galen said. "but no way to tell until we get closer."

"Trouble is, we don't want to get too close," he said, "so it's a cat-and-mouse game."

"I texted Levi and told him what the hell's going on, asking him to check the satellite."

"Shit, I forgot they've got satellite," Zack said. "That's absolutely nuts."

"They're running the GPS off my phone," he said, "so they should get details pretty quickly."

"You really like working for Levi, huh?"

"Well, I like working for Bullard and Levi," he said. "The two of them are cut from the same cloth, it seems. They have different styles, but they're both easy to work with."

"I've worked with Bullard off and on but never full-time."

"You might want to check out Levi. He's got a different scenario, and they've got a ton of work right now."

"Yeah, I was wondering about heading over to America," he said. "I've been in Europe a long time."

"Honestly, it sounds like you could use a clean break and a chance to get away from whatever it is that ties you to her."

"Well, there's no tie anymore," Zack said, with a finality that Galen believed. "It was a long time ago, but I guess I didn't quite let it go."

"You need to now, before you're hooked up as the second husband."

"That's not in the cards," he said. "I spent a lot of time back and forth with her. I don't want to get caught up in that all again. She's very manipulative. Not what I want at this stage of life at all."

His tone was dry but no longer holding hurt. That was something at least. "Ouch. She just saw another choice and went after it? Like climbing a ladder to a better life?"

"As far as I can figure, yes. The fact that she married him helped some but not a whole lot."

"Nobody likes cheaters," Galen said, "particularly if you're the one being cheated on."

Zack laughed at that. "It'd be nice if there was another way. Other than being the cheating person."

"Still, it was a long time ago. It's time to let it go, man."

"Hence the question about going to Levi's. I'm done with her and all that drama."

"Good." Just then Galen's phone buzzed. "It's Levi. They are tracking us on satellite."

"Sweet. Can he get us any details on that vehicle in front of us?"

"Says it's a pickup, a smaller one, but he can't give us

anything more than that."

"Still, a small truck matches up with what Gemma saw with our security cams."

"Yep, but the whole thing stinks. How did anybody know we were here at the commune? Nobody followed us from Joe's cabin. I ran a bug check on my truck and at Joe's cabin and our cabins at the commune."

"Me too on Rebecca's cabin."

"So Rebecca calling Gemma, saying she was kidnapped, just makes me wonder if she gave us the information not because she was being kidnapped," Galen stated, "but because she was in cahoots with those guys and wanted to get away from the whole deal."

"Don't worry. I wondered it myself," Zack said harshly.

Galen looked over at him. "It will break Gemma's heart if her sister is involved like that. Gemma's all heart, and Rebecca is all bitch from what I can see. Of course she doesn't want to be here, and I'm seeing her not at her best," he admitted. "Maybe under different circumstances I'd think she was fine."

"For a long time I didn't think Gemma had a heart," Zack said with a laugh. "But I've come to realize she's got far more heart than her sister does. At the time, I was listening to Rebecca's vitriol, and, if there's one thing Rebecca can't stand, it's competition. She has to knock all other women close to her. I worry about her relationship with Becky later."

"I do too," he said. "Sounds like Gemma's family life was pretty rough with the younger sister being the perfect one. So Gemma chose to spend her summers up here. As soon as she managed to get here the first time, she insisted on coming back every summer thereafter. Until she left her childhood home."

"I can see that. I only know what the sisters told me about their parents. Snobby. Very self-centered and all about appearances. They were likely delighted to get rid of her for a few months. They were all about themselves."

"Just like their youngest daughter."

"Exactly like Rebecca," he said. "And, just like Joe, I wasn't blind to her faults, but somehow they didn't seem to matter."

"And now?"

"Now I've learned an awful lot about life and have had several other relationships," Zack said. "Now I can see how different she is, and it's not the kind of *different* I would choose to spend time with."

"Good," Galen said, and he sure as hell hoped his buddy meant it. "Of course, traveling to the US would be good too. New jobs, new chance to get out, to see new faces, to meet new people."

"Find another long-term girlfriend, you mean," Zack said with a laugh. "I'm okay, you know? It's been really good to see Rebecca through this and to realize just how much I don't want to be with her."

"Good for you," Galen said with a nod. "And I've realized just how much I do want to spend time with Gemma," he said, laughing. "Didn't expect that."

"From what Bullard was saying about Levi's group, maybe you should have. It sounds like everybody else on his team has found a partner."

"They have," Galen said. "Maybe that's one of the reasons why you should come too. Maybe you'll find somebody who's worthy of you."

"Maybe, but I'm not looking," Zack said cheerfully.

Up ahead of them the vehicle slowed and nearly came to

a stop, before it took a left-hand turn.

"I've got it up on GPS," Galen said. "This is going back to Joe's cabin, I think. Not too many driveways on this map. Hardly any side roads to choose from."

They followed a few minutes behind, knowing if they got too close they'd be seen. The moonlight would reflect off their vehicle. As soon as they turned the corner up ahead, they could see the vehicle taking yet another turn.

"Interesting," Zack murmured. "So they left Joe's cabin with Rebecca and looped around back to it again? Was that supposed to get us off their trail? Like, if we had searched Joe's cabin once already, we wouldn't return?" He shook his head as he pulled off the side into the trees and parked the truck, as they watched as the line of vehicle lights headed down through the trees on the opposite side of the road.

"Like I said, going back to Joe's cabin, just from the back way maybe."

"What are you thinking?"

"We go on foot," Galen said.

The two of them got out of the vehicle and quickly geared up. They raced down crosswise, intersecting the road. They didn't say a word; they just picked up the pace. Using the moonlight to help guide them, they made their way through the trees.

When they finally came abreast of a road, Galen said, "It's a dirt road and not very well traveled."

"No, but they went down this way," Zack said. He pointed up ahead where the lights had stopped moving, but they were still shining. Sticking to the trees, they came up behind the vehicle to see that somebody was at the front door of Joe's small cabin, unlocking it.

They watched as the passenger door to the small truck

opened, and Rebecca hopped out. "Hurry up," she snapped.

One of the men looked at her and sneered.

She glared at him.

"What's the matter?" he asked. "Are you missing your beauty sleep?"

"You guys didn't have to force me to come here," she said. "You don't have any idea what kind of trouble you've got me into now."

"You didn't have to put out an SOS call to tell them we were kidnapping you. Just wait until they find out your involvement in this."

"I didn't have any involvement with this," she snapped in a shout. "How many times do I have to tell you that!"

"Well, enough times until we believe you because we sure as hell don't now." The guy walked around the small truck, grabbed her arm roughly, and said, "Come on. Let's go in."

She shrugged him off and headed up the steps. When she got there, the door opened, and she was moved inside. The door shut behind them, and the guy who opened the door came back out to the vehicle, shut it off, and grabbed a bag from inside. He returned to the cabin.

In the darkness, Zack and Galen looked at each other.

"This is still so damn confusing," Galen said with a frown.

"Isn't it?" Zack said, his tone mystified. "And so typical of Rebecca that I'm afraid she's playing one side against the other."

"But you know what always happens to the person in the middle?" Galen said quietly. "They usually get snuffed out permanently."

Chapter 11

MARSHMALLOWS CONSUMED, BECKY curled up in her bed—a very tired, almost teary, little girl—now sound asleep.

Gemma sat in the living room beside the fire with a cup of tea. When her phone buzzed, she lifted it to see it was Galen. She answered it. "Any luck?"

"We found your sister."

"Oh, thank God," she cried out softly. "Is she okay?"

"Well, that's a good question," he said. "We don't have her yet, but she's back in Joe's cabin in the woods. We've just come upon it right now. She's not necessarily been kidnapped, and they seem to think that she was involved. She says she's not involved. We're a little on the confused side."

"And that sounds like Rebecca totally," Gemma said, sighing heavily. "I would hope she had nothing to do with all this, but honestly, I've always been a little worried."

"Well, she wasn't forced into the cabin, but I don't think they would have let her leave on her own."

"That sounds confusing," she said, reaching up to pinch her nose. Why was nothing easy with her sister?

He told her about the little bit of a conversation they had overheard.

She shook her head. "That doesn't say anything, does

it?"

"No. But they seemed to think she contacted us and that she did it deliberately."

"Well, of course she did. I'm her sister. Who else would she call if she's in trouble?" Gemma said. "Besides, outside of grief and shock and reaching out to her only family, why else would she have called me? And asking for help doesn't mean Rebecca is responsible for anything else in this mess."

"Exactly. We're trying to get close enough to hear their conversations," he said, "so I'll let you know if we find out any more."

"Are you bringing her back?"

"Yes, of course," he said, "but we really need to get to the bottom of this first." And, with that, he hung up.

She stared down at the phone in dismay. It was so typical of her sister. She couldn't even be kidnapped in a clean way. Gemma sat here rocking herself, her arms wrapped around her knees, as she wondered what all this meant. She picked up her phone and quickly sent her sister a text. **Are you okay?**

No. Of course I'm not okay. Is the cavalry coming?

At that, Gemma tossed the phone on the couch and stared at it. Should she even tell her sister that the cavalry is coming? Because, if Rebecca had anything to do with this, she would just get Zack and Galen in trouble. And *that* Gemma didn't want to do.

It seemed like every man she knew fell in love with Rebecca. Gemma hoped that Zack had woken up and understood who and what Rebecca was, but it still wasn't a crime to fall under her sister's charms. Zack might have been foolish to fall in love with her sister a long time ago, but that just made him male. And he certainly didn't deserve dying over it now. He'd come here to help them, and Gemma had set this into play.

Thinking about that, she got out her laptop with the video camera feeds and studied that. Her phone buzzed again. She checked to see a text from her sister, with a single question mark, asking for her answer. And, once again, Gemma chose not to respond.

Studying the laptop screens, she found where the two men went into the cabin and partially escorted her sister out. She now understood what Galen had been talking about. Rebecca went on her own, but Gemma doubted that her sister could have left on her own. Gemma frowned, trying to get a closer look at the faces. One of them was definitely somebody she had seen with Joe at work. The same guy who had been in the backyard, trying to gain entry twice to Rebecca's house in the wee hours of the morning. The other guy she didn't know at all. She studied his face, but she couldn't get a closer look at it.

She sent Galen a quick text that one of the kidnappers was the guy who had been involved in the attempted break-in at Joe's house.

Galen texted back his thanks. She smiled at that, wondering at her reluctance to answer her sister. She waited in the darkness with her tea, listening for any sound. And then came a buzz from her phone. She picked it up. Galen calling her. When she put the phone against her ear, he whispered, "We're coming in."

"Okay." She hopped up and stepped outside onto the veranda and walked around to the back door. In the back of the cabin in the distance, she saw lights. She walked out to the parking spot, and he pulled up right in front of her. She looked at him in surprise, not seeing Zack.

Galen hopped out and faced her, talking quietly. "It's just me, and we've got a problem."

"What's that?"

"We overheard an argument they had with your sister. They're demanding ransom," he said.

She raised her eyebrows slowly. "For what?"

"For the return of your sister."

She shook her head. "And is my sister involved in this?"

"Again, I can't tell you that," he said.

She stared at him, in shock. "And just how am I supposed to get ransom out here?"

He took a slow, deep breath. "The ransom they want is Becky."

GALEN DIDN'T KNOW how to tell Gemma that, while he was listening, the kidnappers had made it very clear to Rebecca that they wanted Becky.

Rebecca had screamed, ranted, raved. "No way!"

"That's fine," they had said. "We'll just keep you here until we get Becky."

"No way!" Rebecca shouted.

At that point in time, he and Zack had split up, and Galen came racing here. He walked with Gemma back into the cabin. "I'm here to make sure she stays safe."

"Of course she'll be safe." She hurried ahead of him to where the little girl was sleeping. When she stepped out of the bedroom, she nodded. "She's there."

He could feel the relief instantly relax some of his tension. "Good," he said. "You said a guy was here earlier?"

She nodded. "And, of course, Rebecca disappeared just before that. But we were up at the gardens with Becky."

"So they took the mom and left the daughter behind," Galen said. "But why would they want Becky?" He stared at Gemma for a long moment. "I think it goes back to who her father really is."

Chapter 12

GEMMA'S HEART SANK, and she sat on the steps at the front of the cabin, hoping not to wake Becky or to have her overhear this conversation.

"Rebecca never would tell me," she said softly. "I asked, pleaded, and begged, but she never said. I have to admit to wondering, in my bitchiest moments, if Rebecca didn't know because she had too many possible candidates."

"Did you think it was Zack?"

"I had no clue. I'd really hoped it was Joe."

"So you don't know?"

"No," she said. "I have no idea. Is that why you think they're after Becky?"

Galen nodded slowly. "I don't know what other reason there could be," he said quietly. "Generally, if somebody does this, and they wanted the child as ransom, it's to make the parent fall in line somehow or because they want the child."

"God." She rocked herself on the top step.

He muttered an oath and sat down beside her. Wrapping his arms around her, he pulled her close.

She wasn't normally the type to depend on anybody, but, in that moment, it felt really good to be held. She burrowed in deeper, while his arms crushed her close. "We don't have time for this," she muttered.

"Sometimes you have to take the time when it comes," he said. "Nothing else we can do right now, besides keep Becky safe and figure out who her father is."

"What about the other option? You said something about, if they had Becky, the kidnappers could keep my sister in line."

"Does your sister have direct access to any large sums of money?"

Gemma shook her head. "I don't think so."

"Access to the brewery's business accounts?"

She again shook her head. "I don't think so."

"Did she know anybody else in the company?"

She stopped and looked up at Galen. "Wait. One guy she used to talk about all the time. James. Joe just kind of winced whenever his name came up. I saw him do it."

"Who is this James?"

"According to Rebecca, he was one of the big shareholders for the brewery, but he wasn't in Germany. I think he was in the US."

"Any idea who he is, who he really is?"

She shook her head. "No. But we should be able to figure it out from the company website."

He released her, and together they stood and went back inside. She brought up her laptop and then frowned. "The internet sucks here."

"I know it. We've got a special satellite booster," he said. "Come over here." He hooked up her laptop and said, "We've got a little bit of internet signal here, not too much though."

She quickly checked the company that Joe had worked for. "Here it is," she said. "The list of shareholders. There's a James."

"So maybe that's him?"

She shrugged. "I never heard a last name for him, so maybe. But ..." She turned to face Galen. "His last name is the same as Joe's. *Clark.* Joe Clark. James Clark."

Galen tilted his head. "Common last name. Doesn't necessarily mean they are related. Where is he located?"

"Doesn't say," she said. "It's just his name."

He started searching the net and also asked for information on this James Clark guy from Levi. "And this doesn't mean anything other than James is a common first name that I heard from her lips."

"Right," he said, "but that's something. It's information we haven't had to date." Levi contacted him quickly with an ID and a location. "He's out of Florida," he said. "Miami."

"That's possible," she said with a shrug.

"I have no idea." On his laptop he brought up a face and nodded. "Do you recognize him?"

She looked at it and frowned. "Yes," she said. "I saw a picture of him with my sister."

"When?"

She shook her head. "It was in my sister's purse. She snatched it from my hand and glared at me."

"So it's possible they had a relationship?"

"It's also possible it was just a photo," she retorted. "Not everybody is in love with my sister."

He studied her for a long moment. "No," he said, "not everybody is. I'm certainly not. But she seems like the type to attract lovers and leave the pathways strewn with them."

"Yes," she said. "She is like that." And how interesting that Galen saw through Rebecca so easily. It made him a special kind of man.

"Is there any chance she might have let him think that

Becky was his?"

"I don't know," she cried out in frustration. "Whatever she did is between her and whoever she did it with. I've deliberately distanced myself from my sister when it comes to her relationships."

"Good choice," he said. "That's the safe thing to do. But now we have to figure out who the father is."

"That doesn't matter," she said wearily. "What matters is who *thinks* they are the father."

"True." He stared at her for a long moment. "In your heart of hearts, who do you think is the father?"

"Joe," she said. "Joe and Becky both have the same birthmark on the back of their shoulder. But that still doesn't mean that some other people don't think they are her father too."

Galen kept doing his research, then made an odd sound.

She looked at him. "What?"

He turned around his laptop and said, "Get this. Joe and James are brothers."

She stared at the picture with a sinking heart and whispered, "Shit."

"And based on this," he said, "do you still think Joe is Becky's father?"

She looked up at him, struck dumb for a moment. "They're not only brothers by name," she said, "but they look like brothers. So, no, I can't be sure. Not now."

He nodded, as he kept looking. His phone rang. It was Zack. "What's going on, Zack?"

"Looks like they've turned in for the night," he said. "I did get a photo of one of them. I'm sending it now." He quickly sent it over, and Galen pulled it up on his phone, then turned and faced Gemma with it. "What about this face?"

"The picture's not so great, but it looks similar to James's shareholder photo online and resembles Joe too," she said. "So I presume that's the same James Clark then?"

"Could be—or a thousand other nondescript guys," he said. "And it could very well be that Joe wasn't killed for anything to do with the company but that his brother took him out." She stared at him in horror, and he nodded slowly. "You know yourself about love-hate relationships."

She winced. "Is it that obvious? I really don't like discussing my past."

He gave her a ghostly smile. "No, not at all," he said, "but believe me, I understand. I had a couple relationships that, in hindsight, made me wonder where my head had been at the time. I don't fall easily. In both of those cases, I jumped. As soon as my head cleared, I realized that *lust* had been mistaken for *love*. I'd been lonely and had made up a story that seemed to suit. But it was a story in my head and had nothing to do with the real-life circumstances around me."

"Ditto, although I hadn't thought of it that way. We really do write a story around us, and God help us when we reach the punch line."

He chuckled at that.

She smiled slowly. "So what do we do now?"

"Well, first, we'll have to rescue your sister, and we'll have a plain talk with her," he said. "And then we've gotta figure out how to keep her safe. Honestly, it's not her as much as it's Becky who we need to keep safe."

"So what's next?"

He sighed, stood, and said, "I'm heading back to Zack because we need to set up a mission. You stay here and look after your niece. I'll have a talk with Tim before I leave." He walked over and, in a surprise move, kissed her gently on the temple. She stared at him, wordless. He shrugged. "Stay safe until I get home, will you?"

"Of course," she said faintly. "Why the kiss?"

"I don't know," he said. "Because it felt right, I guess." When she gave him that deep stare again, he laughed and said, "Keep looking at me that way, and I'll do it again."

She shook her head. "It's not the time. This isn't about you. It isn't about me," she said. "And, yes, it is about Rebecca, but, yes, more than that, it's about Becky," she said slowly. "We need to do whatever we can to keep her safe and not get sidetracked with other issues."

"Even if those other issues look really promising?"

She gave him a ghost of a smile. "Especially then."

GALEN HATED TO leave Gemma, and, if he hadn't had a quiet conversation outside with Tim, Galen wouldn't have left. He was confident that Tim would keep an eye on her. He understood the man's mind-set about staying away from society and about avoiding all the ugliness that came with it. But Galen also understood that Tim had a previous military career and had seen the worst of the worst. If he said that he would look out for Gemma and Becky, then he would. Galen was still a little concerned about the heavy artillery on site, but, considering what he would want for himself, if he lived out in a place like this, maybe not so much.

As he drove back along the pathway, he called Zack. "Have they sent out any demands?"

"I don't know," he said, his voice tired. "I don't have any way to tell. I couldn't hear any conversations now, but it could have been done through email, text, or even a notice to the newspaper. I just don't know."

"And who would they send it to?"

"Presumably the newspaper, the brewery, or Joe's family. I'm not sure."

"Are you sure Gemma didn't get a notice?"

"I just spoke to Gemma, and she didn't say anything."

"It could still be coming," Zack said. "Even for instant delivery, out here, with the sparse internet connectivity, any email could be delayed. However, any email can be sent later, to seemingly shift the time zone."

"Well, it's something you and I would do," Galen said. "But them?"

"I'm not sure," he said. "It's obvious we've got some sort of family dynamic going on here."

"And some kind of a lost-lovers' reunion," Galen said sadly. "I don't even know if Rebecca understands what she's wrought on her sister and her own daughter, not to mention all the men involved with her constant lover-on-a-string scenarios."

Zack answered, "I doubt it. She's very good at keeping us on a string."

Zack's voice got to Galen. And how Zack had used the word *us* in his comment too. "Did you cut that string yet?"

"Oh, yeah," Zack said. "Now I'm just sitting here, wondering how I could have been such a fool for all those years."

"But not recently though, right?"

"No, not recently. I hadn't really seen the *Rebecca effect* until now, as I look at these other men and realize how much chaos she's put them through."

"All from a woman who was supposedly married *till death do us part.*"

123

"Which is where the problem comes in because Joe is, of course, dead now," Zack said.

"Did you know him?"

"Yes. Not well, but I did. I hated him at the beginning because she had the affair with him to get away from me."

"Not to get away from," Galen corrected. "Just to move up a rung."

Zack laughed. "Yeah, she's definitely a social climber, isn't she?"

"Absolutely," Galen said. "And she's using her body to get there. You've seen women like that the world over. It's the oldest game in the book, and it won't change anytime soon. Well, until the inevitable aging takes over."

"Right, but she's brought her daughter into this mess, and that's not okay. She can go screw all the men she likes," Zack said forcibly, "but she has no damn business bringing that little girl into it."

"The only constant sanity in Becky's life appears to be Gemma. Joe too, while he was alive."

"You've got to wonder how two women could be so different," Zack said.

"Gemma started looking after her sister by herself at what age? Like seventeen or something?"

"Yeah," Zack replied. "And Rebecca was already well versed in playing the love game by then."

"How old was she when you came on the scene?"

"Eighteen," Zack said. "Joe was the same year."

"And Joe was quite a bit older than you, correct?"

"Depends on what you call *quite a bit*. I'm twenty-eight now, and he was like thirty-four or so. And Rebecca is now twenty-six or twenty-seven, I think," Zack said. "Definitely old enough to know better."

"And old enough to play the odds and to think that she has time left in her life to move up, if something doesn't work out here soon enough," Galen said slowly.

"True, but she's also had plenty of time to get enough data on her target to see if it's worthwhile or not. And to tweak it so that it's perfect."

Galen almost laughed at that. As long as Zack was detached and calm about the whole thing, it did help to see this in a very different light. "So we've got a Lolita here, her little girl with uncertain paternity, and several men who we presume are thinking they could be the father. But what does it all mean?" Galen asked as he rubbed his face in frustration.

"Do you think that's why the kidnappers want Becky?" Zack asked.

"I would hope so," Galen said. "It would be damn sad if it were for another power play."

"What kind of power play?" he asked.

"Well, if it's James, and he thinks Becky is his own daughter, I would hope that he would want to protect her and not send her off into the sex trade or something. But, if he doesn't think it's his daughter, and he's just looking to punish the mother, that brings up all kinds of horrible scenarios."

There was a long moment before Zack spoke. "You really didn't have to voice that, you know?"

"Actually, I did," he said. "We can't hide anymore from these elements," he said. "The potential here is way too serious."

"I get you," he said, "but it sucks."

"I'm just a few minutes away. Any update on what's going on inside the cabin?"

"As far as I can see," Zack said, "they've all gone to bed."

"Well, here's a question for you," he asked. "Was everybody in a separate bed?"

"Last I saw them? Yes," he said, "but that doesn't mean there hasn't been some nighttime shuffling."

"Given that she might need a way out of this, that would be one avenue to make it happen."

"I think I'll check the bedrooms," he said.

"You do that. I should be around the house pretty quick."

Galen hung up the phone, tossed it onto the seat beside him, and pulled into the same place he had parked last time. He shut off the engine and sat here, waiting. When he figured it was safe, he slipped out and slid through the trees, heading toward the cabin. His mind still tumbled with the possibilities of what was going on and could only hope that things came to a head pretty damn quick.

As he headed toward where Zack was last, Galen stopped and studied the cabin. He saw no signs of movement and no signs of any life on the inside. The only thing that bothered him was he also saw no signs of life on the outside either.

Where was Zack?

Chapter 13

HOW THE HECK was Gemma supposed to sleep with all this going on? She kept her eye on the laptop and one on the book in her hand, as she sat in front of the fire in the main room as the wee hours of the night passed by. She got up what seemed like every thirty minutes to check on Becky. Gemma wished that she could sit beside Becky or that the little girl could move out to the couch with her. The bedrooms in these small cabins were pretty much taken up by the bed in each. No room to even drag in a spare chair. Gemma could join Becky on the bed. She had contemplated doing that but didn't want to wake her. At least one of them should get some sleep on this dark night.

When she heard a cracking sound outside, she immediately slipped over to the window. Just being where they were, it could have been wildlife. They were still inside the fence of the compound, but that wouldn't stop a coyote. And, if it was a fox coming in after the hens, he would have come in from the far side. At least she thought so, but she wasn't a fox, so who knew?

Another crackle came, and her breath caught in the back of her throat as she studied the darkness outside. She was tucked up against the curtain, so, if it was a two-legged predator, she had no way of staying hidden, except by staying out of the light of the fireplace from the inside and out of the moonlight from the outside.

When the sound faded away again, she relaxed. But, just as she settled on the couch again, she heard something on the other side of the cabin. Swearing softly, she got up and walked to the other window. The curtains were closed so she lifted a corner to peer outside and could see a man standing there, as he studied the space between the two cabins. She sucked in her breath, until she realized it was one of Tim's men. And then she had to wonder. Why was he here? He did have a weapon tucked in the back of his pocket, and he also held a rifle.

When a call came from the far side of the acreage, he answered it. She smiled, realizing it was the sentry. Was this new? She didn't remember seeing anything like this when she had been here as a child and later as a teen. But then her life had changed, and being a child was no longer an option in this world. Gone was her sense of innocence, of not knowing how the actual world worked. Just because her family scenario was crap, she'd always been optimistic that the rest of the world functioned in a much saner and more positive way.

As she watched, the man walked to Rebecca's cabin, checked inside again, and then headed across toward the long house. She walked to the front window and studied him as he hopped up onto the veranda of the long house and calmly walked into the front door. Definitely a sentry then.

When her phone buzzed, she snatched it off the back of the couch. *Tim.* Sending her a message that all was well. She smiled and quickly answered. **I wondered when I saw somebody walking around the cabins.**

We're doing constant patrols. Particularly now.

Is this new?

Yes. Galen asked us specifically to keep an eye on you, but we would have anyway.

She smiled at that and sent him a heart emoji. Tim was a good guy. He didn't really want any of this kind of thing in his world, and she appreciated that he'd opened the door for them as it was. And he wouldn't have done it if she hadn't have been one of the people who had been here summer after summer after summer. She really appreciated what he was doing. She sent him a quick note of thanks.

When no response came, she returned to the couch with her phone and watched the fire. Her fingers itched to send Galen a message, but she didn't want to disturb him. Plus, if he didn't have his phone muted or off, it would potentially let somebody know he was there, and she didn't want to risk anything like that.

As she lay on the couch, she couldn't help but think about how life had switched for her right now. She'd taken time off work to deal with this. Seemed her boss was afraid she would quit, even suggesting she spend more time at home. She wondered about doing that, but she was only half interested in the suggestion. She would need to find a home where she was happy to stay.

She had an apartment in New York but hated it. It was dark and dreary, and getting out anywhere without a million or more people around was hard. She yearned for open spaces again. Being here at the compound had reminded her that her heart still loved the country. She would have loved an acre or more to herself with a house in the middle, nicely fenced to keep out the world. Of course that wouldn't keep out any predator intent on getting in, but it was likely the best she could do.

She didn't know what Galen's story was. They hadn't

had a chance to talk, but that little kiss had been very telling, and, if she were honest, she wanted to spend more time with him. She hadn't been in a relationship in a long time, and mostly she kept herself too busy. After watching her sister treat men like objects, Gemma never wanted anybody to treat her like one as well.

With her parents, her sister, and her ex-fiancé, Gemma had come away with a very different view of how relationships worked and what she wanted for herself. She wanted something based on mutual trust, where she didn't have to worry about her partner flirting all the time with other women. She wanted to grow old together in the two rocking chairs on the front deck, just like Tim and his partner Mary were.

Gemma hadn't seen much of Mary since their arrival here, except for a quick moment saying hi in the kitchen. She knew a lot of society would look down on that relationship because Mary was the epitome of the old pioneer woman. The thing is, Mary was happy, she was doing what she loved doing. She loved getting up at four o'clock in the morning, baking the bread for the compound. She loved puttering in her garden and picking peas for dinner.

If there was one thing Gemma had come to learn in all those summers she had spent here, it was that some people wanted things for themselves that other people couldn't understand, and it wasn't for Gemma to judge. It wasn't for her to think that they were wrong—unless they were harming themselves and/or others—and it should be all about understanding that each person had different needs and wishes for their own life.

Gemma had come to the crux of the matter right now and realized that she wanted something different for herself too.

When she heard a strangled cry from the bedroom, she jumped to her feet and raced into the little room. In there, she could see Becky tossing in the bedcovers. Gemma immediately sat down on the side of the bed and stroked her niece's cheek, pushing the sweaty tendrils of hair off her face. "It's all right, sweetie. Aunt Gemma's here."

Becky opened her eyes and stared up at her, then yawned and snuggled deeper into the pillow.

Gemma smiled and just kept stroking her niece's head until the little girl calmed down again and drifted off to sleep without saying a word.

This is what I want, Gemma thought, *a family. Children.* Maybe not today, maybe not tomorrow, but somewhere along the line, she wanted to have a Becky of her own. Not for the reason that Rebecca had, but because Gemma wanted someone to love and to be loved by. This little girl had a special place in her heart. But it said something about Rebecca as a mother that she gave her baby exactly the same name she had herself. Typically things like that were reserved for middle names for females. But Rebecca had named her baby Rebecca. And not given her another name.

Gemma had found that self-serving at the time, but Rebecca had said Gemma was being ridiculous. Her daughter would be a perfect replica of her, so she needed to have her name too. It had been all Gemma could do to choke back the harsh words, but, when she thought about the number of parents who named their kids after grandparents, she wondered if it was wrong at all. It would just add confusion when they were both adult women, but, in the end, they called little Rebecca *Becky* all the time, so it didn't seem to matter now. By then, Becky would be old enough to take things into her own hands and to make decisions for herself.

Who was she to argue? She was *Gemma*. She'd been called Gem by more than a few friends but was often just straight Gemma.

When the little girl was comfortable again, Gemma sank onto the couch, and, in spite of her wishes to stay awake, she could feel herself dozing off. She'd long since run out of hot drinks, and a trip to the outhouse was something she didn't want to do while she was looking after the sleeping little girl. She should have gone when the sentry was here. But her bladder was getting extremely insistent. She frowned, wondering how long she could hold off. She looked at her phone for the umpteenth time, wondering when Galen would get in touch. If he was home, she'd make the trip, but she didn't want to leave Becky alone.

Finally her bladder wouldn't give her any option. She slipped to the rear door and took the twenty steps to the outhouse farther back. That was likely why Rebecca was totally against coming here. No indoor plumbing for the cabins. Not that Gemma herself cared, but Rebecca considered it offensive. The long house had indoor plumbing, and most likely for all the other cabins, but these two were just overflow cabins. She quickly took care of business and returned to the little cabin.

As she approached the bottom step, somebody grabbed her from behind and slapped a hand over her mouth. She shrieked, but no sound came out. She sent an elbow her attacker's way a couple times, while also kicking him with her boot, and grabbed the hand holding her, digging in her nails, fighting, until she heard a voice whispering in her ear.

"Calm down. It's me."

She stopped fighting him the second she heard his voice.

Realizing it was Galen, she sagged in place.

He slowly lifted his hand from her mouth. "We're getting company, so I need you to stay quiet."

And she froze.

GALEN HADN'T WANTED to scare Gemma, but he needed her to stay quiet. He should have expected her to have some decent fighting skills, and she'd certainly caught him with a couple decent blows with her boot and her elbow, and she'd actually cut the skin on the back of his hands with her nails. But he hadn't wanted to hurt her, so he'd taken it and had not made a sound. He let her into the cabin and shut the rear door silently. He pulled her close, crushing her against his chest.

"I just went to the outhouse. I couldn't wait any longer," she said, as her arms wrapped around him.

"I understand that. We need to check that Becky is still in the bedroom."

She took one look at him, the whites of her eyes glowing in the dark. She looked at the bedroom and shook herself free of his arms.

Instantly, the two of them moved, tiptoeing as quietly as they could. She sighed with joy when she saw that Becky was still here. When he confirmed that she was sleeping, he reached out for Gemma and just held her close.

"Who's here?" she breathed the words against his ear.

"Not sure," he whispered. "When I got back to Zack, I found him knocked out on the ground outside Joe's cabin, and the others were missing."

She reared back and stared at him in shock.

"I brought Zack along, but he's still out cold in the back

of the truck."

She shook her head, her hand covering her mouth. "Dear God."

He nodded. "I know. This is getting ugly."

"We have to tell Tim."

"I did. I sent him a text." He lightened his grip, but, when her shoulders sagged, he tucked her up close again. When she snuggled in deeper, he just smiled and hugged her tight.

"What are we doing here?"

"Waiting for them to come after Becky." She stiffened in his arms, but there was no help for it. She had to know the truth. He just held her close as he let her process the information.

"Do you think my sister's here?"

"I don't know," he said. "I left Zack down on the ground to head to Joe's cabin, to ensure that all three were still in separate bedrooms, like they were not ten minutes earlier when I last spoke with Zack. But, before I even reached the cabin, their vehicle took off. I picked up Zack and loaded him in the back of our truck and followed, tracking them here. They're parked down on the far side in the bushes, and I'm even farther out. So I know that they were coming here, which means your sister has talked."

Gemma winced at that. "She must be desperate."

"I think, at the moment, she's playing the odds to get out of here safely." His voice was as low as he could make it. "But that's no guarantee that anybody will get out of this alive."

"Tim's sentries have weapons," she said.

He nodded, saying, "But so did these guys."

She stared up at him and shook her head mutely. "We

can't have Tim's guys getting hurt."

"I'm not planning on it," he said, "but I know that the bad guys are coming here after Becky, and, if you're here, you're also in the line of fire. You and that little girl are my priorities." With that said, he pulled her back a little farther so they were in the dark corner in the rear of the cabin.

She looked around. "They could come in through the window in that room."

"I'm guessing they figure they'll have to take you out first," he said. "They don't know where I am, but, since they found Zack, they'll know that I'm around somewhere."

"Rebecca could have told them," she said instantly. "And, even if she didn't, they would have checked her phone, finding the text where she asked me if the cavalry was coming."

"The cavalry?"

"Yes," she said, "and I didn't answer."

He nodded. "She also knows you though. She expects, if there was any way for us to come after her, that you would send us."

"That's what I figured."

Just then they heard several footsteps outside. He gripped her tight and pulled her closer. "Don't move," he whispered. He drew his gun from his holster and kept the weapon at the side of his thigh, waiting. He had no problem shooting to kill. He could only hope that Tim didn't have a problem disposing of the body or leaving it someplace where the cops could find it a long way away from here.

When they heard more footsteps, she spun in his arms and whispered, "Don't shoot. It could be Tim or one of his men."

He disagreed. "Or possibly your sister?"

She nodded. "I think so."

They waited and heard one more step up, the wood creaking gently under the weight. He wondered, if it was the sister, why she was coming up so slowly? The front door opened, and he saw the shape, definitely female. But there was also a weapon. He could feel Gemma stiffen in his arms as she saw it as well. And then she sucked in her breath.

"Gemma, you here?" Rebecca called out.

He squeezed Gemma tight, and she stayed silent.

"Goddammit. Come on, Gemma. Are you here? I need help."

At that, Gemma looked up at him. He shook his head.

"I swear, if you've taken off without me," she said, "I'll be so pissed."

"Are they in there?" asked a man from outside.

Galen smiled at that because now somebody had shown their hand. Gemma stiffened in outrage.

"I can't see her," Rebecca snapped. "Now that you've fucking told the world that you're here …"

"I'm just trying to help," he said.

"Check the other cabin," she hissed. She stepped inside, her eyes slowly adjusting to the dark.

They were just barely hidden, and, as soon as Rebecca came around looking for Becky, she'd see them.

She walked forward a few feet. "Why is there a goddamn fire? What'd you do, fall asleep?" she muttered. "Bloody country nightmare this is." She hurried into the bedroom. As soon as she saw her daughter, she cried out and raced toward her. All Galen could see was her shadowy figured bending over Becky, but the gun stuffed in the back of Rebecca's waistband was clearly evident. But, when she scooped up her daughter, completely wrapped up in blankets, and she headed for the front door, he let Gemma go. She immediately raced to the front door and stood in the way.

"Where are you going?" Gemma asked.

"What were you doing, sleeping on the goddamn floor?" Rebecca said in outrage. "I called out. Where were you?"

"Sleeping obviously," Gemma said smoothly. "What are you doing?"

"I'm taking her out of here," she said. "This was a shitty idea in the first place."

"So are you taking her away from the kidnappers or toward them?" Gemma asked quietly. "I guess what I'm really asking is if you're handing her over to the people who wanted her as ransom, so you can go free and clear. Or are you trying to run from yet another man who thinks he's the father of your child? Which is it?"

Galen shifted silently to get a better look at Rebecca. He saw her features twist. First with shock, then with fury. And finally with malice. There really wasn't anything Galen liked about this damn woman.

Chapter 14

"**W**ELL?" GEMMA SAID quietly. "So you brought somebody here with you. One of your supposed kidnappers, I presume?"

Glaring, her arms straining from carrying Becky, Rebecca said, "Move. This has nothing to do with you, Gemma."

"Well, obviously it does," Gemma said. "I don't know how this is all supposed to play out or what you hope to get out of it, but I did this to help you and Becky."

"Your help was never wanted," Rebecca sneered. "Ever. All you do is interfere."

"Right," Gemma said, trying to stifle the hurt. "Maybe you'd like to elaborate."

"No, I sure wouldn't," she said, struggling now under the strain of carrying the sleeping child. "What I want you to do is get the hell out of my way."

"Mommy?"

Gemma looked down to see Becky gazing at her mother, a frown on her face.

"Oh, good, you're awake," Rebecca said, abruptly putting her on her feet. "Now be quiet."

"What happened? What's going on?" Becky rubbed her eyes as she swayed on her feet.

"I said, be quiet," Rebecca snapped, glaring from her daughter to her sister.

Becky stared up at her mother, then turned to look at Gemma, tears welling up in her eyes.

Gemma smiled at her. "It's okay, sweetheart."

"Of course it's not okay," Rebecca said. "All you ever do is lie and tell kids that it's okay. Nothing is ever okay."

"Maybe you should explain that too," Gemma said quietly. "You're supposedly kidnapped, and now you're here with one of the kidnappers, trying to take your daughter away."

"And that's the part that you just don't seem to understand, Gemma," Rebecca sneered again. "She's *my* daughter, so I get to do what I want. Go have your own instead of trying to live your motherhood through my child."

"Not if it'll hurt her you don't," Gemma said, straightening against her sister's words. Then her sister had always used words as weapons. Gemma should be used to it, but any words that would hurt Becky weren't okay, at any time.

"I'd never hurt her. She's my daughter," she said, with a wave of her hand. "But somebody needs to meet her."

"You mean, the man who thinks he's her father?"

"How do you know, he isn't?" she asked in a snide tone. "You always act like you are better than me. That you know my business. The truth is, you don't know anything."

"If you slept with five guys in the same night, I can see how you wouldn't have a clue about the father," Gemma said, gearing up for one of Rebecca's little fits. "And quite probably, five guys in the same week won't tell you who it is either. But chances are, it will come down between Joe and James, both brothers, who I presume you slept with at the same time that you were sleeping with Zack."

"Zack and I were over at that point in time," she said, with yet another wave of her hand, so casual, as if he didn't even count. "I was done with him a long time before that. But he was useful to keep around."

"You just forgot to tell him, is that it?" Gemma said, trying to infuse a note of humor in the scenario to calm it down.

"Whatever," Rebecca said. "This has nothing to do with him either. He's just a pain in the ass, and I wish he'd disappear."

"Well," Gemma said, "that sounds lovely. And yet he has bent over backward to help you. You called him. Remember?"

"I needed him, and now I don't. And again, I don't need any help," she sneered. "God, you're so simple sometimes, Gemma." She fluttered her hand around the cabin. "Look at this place. It's disgusting. I'm not staying here another night."

"And that's got nothing to do with the kidnapping or the kidnappers," Gemma said, taking a step to the door, preventing her sister from bolting outside.

"Get out of my way," Rebecca roared.

"No," Gemma said, crossing her arms over her chest, leaning against the doorjamb. "Not until you explain what's going on."

"There's nothing to explain," her sister snapped. "You don't understand anything!"

"I do understand you are keeping various men on your string, and you like to pull on those strings, keeping the men jealous of each other. Sure, I understand that. But you haven't explained what this kidnapping is all about."

"Joe was being blackmailed," she said resentfully. "There. Are you satisfied?"

Gemma studied her sister for a long moment. "No. I'm

not satisfied because I'm not sure I believe you. You make up stories on the spot. Maybe you should become a politician," she said humorously.

"I never make up stories," she said. "I call them fibs, and he was being blackmailed."

"Why?"

"It was about the company."

"No. This has nothing to do with the company," Gemma said, standing resolute in front of her sister and waited for the next wave of lies.

Rebecca glared at her in frustration. Finally she gave in. "Fine. He was being blackmailed about Becky. But he had dirt on someone in the company. A ledger. About the embezzlement from his predecessor. He wanted to go over it first, then hand it off to the authorities. He figured the break-ins and the thefts at the company were all connected."

Gemma stared at her sister. Was she telling the truth? There was a ring of it in her words, but that just made her a good liar. However, Becky had mentioned seeing a ledger at home. Possibly the ledger from work. Maybe left behind in Joe's home office, somewhere no one expected it to be found. Except Rebecca could have easily moved it, since Becky saw it last with Rebecca. Who could be blackmailing Joe's predecessor, for all Gemma knew. She didn't know what to think about her sister right now. Or about Joe being blackmailed about Becky. Her take was Rebecca was holding Becky's parentage over Joe's head. That would hurt him terribly if he wasn't the father. But it wouldn't change how he felt about her. Joe had loved Becky. Becky had loved Joe.

"Me?" Becky asked, staring up at her mother in shock. "What did I do?"

"You exist," her mother snapped. "Just be quiet."

Becky took a couple steps off to the side, staring up at her mother, tears in the corner of her eyes. But it was the look on her face that broke Gemma's heart.

"Rebecca, stop talking to Becky that way *now*," Gemma stated in a hard voice. "Becky, come here, sweetie." And she picked her up and drew her close. Becky was pretty upset about this conversation and yet remained such a special girl. Through all of this, she'd stayed sweet. But what she was watching now hurt. It was the loss of innocence. The first awareness of her mother in a new light. Something else Gemma could relate too.

While Rebecca held her tongue, Gemma asked her, "Let's go back to what you said. Do you mean somebody thought Joe wasn't her father, that she was his, and wanted his daughter back?"

Rebecca shrugged. "Maybe."

"Maybe, maybe not. Joe's brother by any chance? Did you actually sleep with his brother?" Oh, dear God. If she'd told Joe, ... the heartache and pain. ... Her sister just couldn't resist destroying anything good around her. It was like a disease, where she couldn't stand for anyone else to be happy. Gemma shook her head as she patted Becky and gently swayed her in her arms.

"Well, I wanted to know if there was anything different about them," she admitted, "but all men are the same. All sex is the same. There's nothing special about any of it."

At that, Gemma tried to cup Becky's ears, but it was basically too late. "It's only about what you can get from it, I presume?"

"Of course. Men are simple. Tools. Everyone knows that. Sex is a business transaction. God, you're so innocent." Her sister's tone of voice was filled with disgust, but, as she'd had a lifetime of practice, Gemma easily ignored it.

"Interesting that's how you view it," Gemma said, filled with sadness. "Is that what your relationship with Joe was like?"

"Of course I used him to make life comfortable and to ensure our needs were met."

"You mean, a fancy house, bank accounts, credit cards, designer clothes, trips, jewelry, and whatever else you might want on the spur of the moment?" The problem was Gemma knew Joe had been happy …

"Of course," she said. "If you weren't so stuck-up and cold, you could have had a boyfriend give you things too."

"Where did you learn that from?" Gemma asked, incredulous though not surprised. "It's hard to believe Mom thought that way about Dad."

"Of course she did," Rebecca said. "She told me to be very careful who I picked for a permanent partner, to make sure they could take me high enough and look after me the way I deserved."

"So what did you decide to do then?" Gemma asked. "Instead of sticking with Joe, you got rid of him so you could go on to the next one?"

"I didn't kill Joe!" Rebecca roared. "How many times do I have to tell you that?"

Just then something poked her in the back of the neck, and Gemma realized she'd been so focused on her sister that she'd completely forgotten about the guy outside.

The gun at her back said that the guy hadn't forgotten her.

"Move into the cabin. Enough of this BS sister crap," the stranger snapped. "And keep your hands where I can see them."

Gemma slowly moved into the cabin, the gun at her neck, her hands secured around Becky, Gemma's body in between Becky and the gunman. Gemma wasn't sure where Galen was, but she was grateful he was here somewhere. When she was deeper inside the cabin, she turned sideways, still protecting Becky, to study the gunman, who even now was relieving Rebecca of the gun hidden at her back. She couldn't help but wonder if that was the same gun that had killed Joe?

Wow. Even this guy doesn't trust Rebecca. "So, you're the man who tried to break into Rebecca's house twice," she said. "So I suppose now you'll tell me that you didn't shoot Joe either? With that gun?" She was desperate for clarity here.

"I was to shoot Joe, and she was part of it." He tilted his head toward Rebecca and smiled. "And yes, this gun."

"I was not. I told you that," she shouted.

"You told me to do what needed to be done," he said. "Don't think you'll get out of this now when your hands are as dirty as mine."

"You weren't supposed to kill him," she said resentfully, glaring at the gunman.

"What were you supposed to do?" Gemma asked the man curiously. Her heart sank as she realized what the turn of events meant for her family's future. If any of them survived this.

"I was supposed to kidnap the little girl and hold her until big daddy-o paid the ransom. And get the damn ledger at the same time and make it look like a robbery, all tied to the brewery." He pointed the gun at Rebecca. "She told me where to find it in his home office."

"Will you keep your damn trap shut!" Rebecca yelled at

the gunman, despite him having both guns.

"Ah." Gemma turned to look at her sister. "So you didn't want to divorce Joe. You wanted to bankrupt him first and then divorce him?" Yet that made no sense either, for her sister loved her creature comforts. She'd get less in a settlement if Joe was broke beforehand. Although it would maximize the pain she inflicted on him.

"Not really," her sister said, looking around, ignoring Gemma to speak to the gunman. "We need to get out of here before anybody comes. Zack and Galen will be lurking here somewhere."

"Yeah, like where is your lover?" Gemma asked. "Joe's brother. I'm sure he's somewhere here too."

At that, there was silence. "What do you know about that?" Rebecca finally said in a shrill voice, glaring at her sister.

"Well, if you were after the ledger, you could blackmail whoever was desperate to find it, take the payout money, and run for a new life, then divorce Joe and take everything you could from him, probably putting your daughter in jeopardy at the same time to twist that screw, and, of course, you'd have another guy to go to. I figured Joe's brother was probably lined up as the right one for the moment."

"As usual, you don't know anything. You're just guessing," her sister snapped in an ugly voice. "And you think you're so damn smart. But you're stupid, always have been. I'm way smarter."

There wasn't any love in her tone or even joy at the idea of now glomming onto James's coattails. *Odd.* It seemed like she had more animosity toward Joe's brother. Interesting. And confusing. Gemma still hadn't quite figured out how this was supposed to work, but she was getting there. She turned to look back at the gunman. "I don't know who you are," she said, then motioned at Rebecca, "but you're both shit for terrorizing a child."

"I didn't terrorize anybody," he said. "I just followed her plan."

"You did not," her sister snapped. Rebecca turned to study Gemma and, in a sly voice, said, "I told you that you should have left us alone, Gemma. But you never listen and always go where you're not wanted."

"Well, I was more concerned about Becky than you were, obviously," Gemma said. "You've always landed on your own two feet. Or somebody else's penis," she said.

The guy with the gun sniggered.

"Is it not the truth?" Gemma said, trying to provoke her sister into telling the truth. How Gemma hated that Becky was hearing all this. But only now did Gemma worry about all the poor child had already been through these last eight years with her mother. "Did Joe know about your activities? Did you break his heart before you shot him? He loved you so much. To know what you are would have killed him without the aid of a bullet."

Rebecca straightened up. "Joe was done with us." Her glare getting even hotter.

Then that was no surprise. Rebecca had a hell of a temper. So maybe now they'd find out the truth. "You mean, you were done with Joe, and you were just looking for your next mark, but, at the same time, you couldn't just leave him heartbroken at you leaving him. You had to twist the knife and let him know you were having affairs all over the place, right?"

"Like I said, it's none of your business, and you don't know anything about it," Rebecca said. "Besides, you wouldn't understand. You've always hated me. I mean, I'm so much prettier and better at dealing with men than you. Your jealousy is understandable but wearing. You've always been like this. The ugly duckling of the family. We couldn't wait to get rid of you, and, like a bad penny, you kept coming back."

"Oh, absolutely," Gemma said with a smile. "I mean, it's not like I've killed any husbands or had affairs where I screwed multiple men in the same night, brothers even. You know what? Where I'm kind of old-fashioned that way, I like to think of one man at a time, whereas you don't care. You don't even know who your daughter's father is," she said, shaking her head. "And that's nothing to be proud of, so keep your high and mighty BS attitude away from me."

"Mother always said you were such a prude."

"Obviously I didn't know them at all," Gemma said. Inside, she was more than a little heartbroken, and yet she shouldn't be. She understood her mother hadn't been anyone she could relate to. It had sent her to bed to cry herself to sleep many nights. It took her a while to realize it wasn't her fault. It was her mother's.

"Well, you should understand that because you're not hers and Daddy's child anyway."

"Yeah, I am," she said. "You might want to think that I don't belong to the family, but you're wrong."

"No. That's not true," she said, as if privy to a secret. "Mom told me."

"Of course she did. She was as much of a liar as you are. That was her way of disassociating from having to look after me as being hers. She never related to me, but we were blood."

"No," she said. "You're just thinking that you are."

"I had the DNA test done, Rebecca," she said. "Dad told me that, if I wanted to, I could, but that I belonged to them. That was after I threw it back at them, saying I wasn't even theirs, after Mom had told me the same thing. He just laughed and said absolutely I was. So I had the test done. It didn't take much, and he paid for it, but then money was never a big thing to him, was it?"

"No, which is one of the reasons Mother was setting up to leave him."

"Ah," she said. Gemma thought back over the years to the car accident. "And Dad was driving. Don't suppose she told him that she was leaving him that same night, maybe in the car, right before they died, huh?"

An odd silence came as Rebecca looked at her. "You're not saying that he killed her, are you?"

"I wouldn't be at all surprised, but it's also possible they had a hell of a fight, and a terrible accident stemmed from that," she said. "When you start wrapping people around and making yourself so dispensable to these people who are lovesick, overwhelmed, and caught up in making your life happen, cutting them loose with that same bitterness, well, it's not hard to imagine that they might snap."

"Well, Joe did," she said resentfully. "He didn't want a divorce, and then he told me that he would let everybody know what I was like."

"Ah. I see. So you had already asked for a divorce. So, more lies. Layers and layers of lies." She looked over at the guy holding the gun on her. "What are you, her next life?"

He shrugged. "I fucked her a few times. It's nothing special. But then getting laid is getting laid."

At that, Rebecca looked at him with a glacial gaze that would have cut him in two if she could have. "Well, you won't be doing it again."

"Until you need something," he said. "One thing about bitches is that you just have to put them to good use. And they're only good for one thing." Then he waved the gun at Gemma. "Still, I got the ledger I was after, so it's all good." He glared at Rebecca. "And it's mine, not yours. Oh, and let's not forget who's holding the gun."

"Oh, absolutely not," Rebecca said with a sneer. "Let's not forget you're the one who broke into my house and stole that ledger and killed my husband."

"Is that your line? We'll see how that works in the future. Besides, you brought the gun that killed him here and kept it for more of your dirty work, but I have it now," he said with a smirk. "Let's not forget that too, sweetheart."

"Doesn't matter," she said. "No judge will believe you over me."

"Well, maybe if we got a female judge," Gemma chimed in, both her and the gunman chuckling at her quip. Relaxing, Gemma shifted with Becky, stepping a little farther back into the cabin, to the side, where she had last been with Galen.

A shot was fired into the cabin, slamming into the wood at the far end. She stared at everybody, for a fraction of a second, grabbed her niece firmly, and dropped to her knees, hit the floor on her back, rolling gently to shield Becky.

GALEN BAILED OUT the bedroom window and came around the back, looking for this guy's partner. But he saw no sign of him. He headed back at a fast clip to the small pickup and found Zack waking up. Galen quickly explained the scenario and sent Zack up to get Tim; then Galen came racing back around the cabin. He didn't know what the hell was going on. That baby sister deserved to be six feet under as far as he was concerned. The little girl, Becky, was a sweetheart, but her mother was a piranha.

Just as he was about to make his move to take out the gunman without getting the women hurt, somebody fired a shot from the far side of the compound. He did an about-face. Now he was tracking through the darkness to find the shooter, praying to God that Gemma and Becky were unharmed.

He heard his phone buzz, likely Zack sending him a message, but he didn't take the time. After a short detour into the trees to hide him, to take in his surroundings, Galen was on the move again. As soon as he approached the area where he thought the shot had come from—which was between the chicken coop and the barn—he slid up against the wall and listened. Up ahead he could hear somebody running through the brush. No one near as quiet or as stealthy as Galen was. Likely another of Rebecca's stooges. And hopefully the last one. Had he been the shooter into the cabin? Had he planned on killing his partner? Or had he finally seen the light with Rebecca?

Or maybe he figured it was all a bad deal, and he just wanted to get rid of them all.

Galen pulled out his phone and checked Zack's message, which said Tim was coming with sentries. He typed a quick note back, alerting Zack to his location. The last thing Galen wanted was to get shot by friendly fire.

Footsteps pounded the ground ahead. Galen went low into the brush and raced after the footsteps. Almost as if the shooter understood he was no longer alone or had heard Galen or maybe just saw a clear path ahead of him, the source of the footsteps broke into a run, and all of a sudden the shooter raced away. Galen picked up speed, and suddenly he heard a vehicle door slam shut and an engine start up.

Swearing to himself, he picked up the pace, going faster and faster in the dark. But it was damn hard to see anything at this hour. He saw the lights up ahead, as a vehicle headed out of its hiding place. He wasn't even sure if it was on a road or if it was stuck on the side of the road. Apparently it wasn't on a road because he watched it do a series of awkward maneuvers, trying to turn around to go in the opposite direction.

Galen came up just as it made a pivot, and he grabbed the driver's door. It swung open, and the driver looked at him, startled. Reaching for a hold on the shooter's jacket, Galen dragged him onto the ground, jumping on top of him, and slamming his fist hard into the guy's temple.

When the man collapsed underneath him, Galen sank on top of his captive, gasping for breath. He pulled out his phone and sent a message to Zack. Quickly he took a photo of the shooter's face and sent that afterward. With the phone in his hand, he called Gemma, who quickly answered.

"I know you have a guy with a gun in there, but you may want to tell him that I've got his partner."

Her voice was calm as she said, "Will do."

God he loved that about her. He could hear her saying, "Yo, gunman, Galen's got your partner and the getaway vehicle."

Galen could hear the man swearing in the background. But his voice was too muffled to hear the conversation.

"No, I don't want to tell him that. If you want to talk to him, here."

Galen heard a muffled sound as she handed over the

phone.

"You bring my partner here," the gunman said, "or I'll start killing people."

"If you kill anybody," Galen said, his voice calm, "you won't live to see morning."

"Says you. I'm the one with the gun."

"Yeah? Well at least ten guys on this place are coming toward you right now. All of them with guns," he said. "So you better use yours wisely. Otherwise you'll get a bullet through the forehead, and nobody'll give a shit out here. We'll use one of these dark old ravines to deep-six your body, and nobody will ever find you. And, yeah, I've got your partner," he said. "Don't worry. I'll be there in a few minutes. Count on it."

And, with that, he hung up. He picked up the guy, tossed him into the backseat of his getaway vehicle, giving him one more punch to the head to make sure he stayed out. Turning the guy's vehicle around, Galen drove slowly back to where he had parked earlier with Zack. Then he dragged out the unconscious man, threw him over his shoulder, and hoofed it down to the cabins.

As soon as he got there, the door opened, and Gemma took one look at him. "Are you okay?" she cried out, as she sat up, still on the floor, seated by Becky, patting the girl, calming her.

He nodded and dumped the second man onto the floor in front of the gunman, who still held his own handgun. In the same calm movement, Galen ripped the gun away from him. "You shouldn't fucking touch these." Reaching up, he brought the barrel of the gun down hard on the bewildered gunman's head.

With an odd look on his face, the man went down next

to his buddy.

Galen promptly searched him, finding a second gun which he also pocketed. Galen looked over at Gemma. "The question is, are you and Becky okay?"

Looking at the two men on the ground, she looked up at him, now standing. "Remind me never to piss you off."

"Sweetheart, you can piss me off all you want," he said. "I would never hit you."

She smiled, walked into his arms, and held him close.

He looked down to see Becky staring at them from the floor, obviously shocked at the sudden turn of events.

He opened his arms and said, "It's okay, sweetheart. Come here."

She raced toward them and wrapped her arms around both of them. Then he turned his gaze to the bitch of a mother. "Well, hello, Rebecca."

She stared at him in shock, then down at the two men on the ground. Immediately her tone of voice changed. "Well, thank God, you got those two men," she cried out, rushing toward him. But his arms didn't open for her. She halted a few steps from them. "Of course I had to say what I said," she told her sister. "You have no idea how they treated me."

"Yeah, I do, Rebecca," Gemma said tiredly. "Give it a break, will you?"

"What are you talking about?"

"I set up electronics at Joe's cabin."

"What are you talking about? What electronics?"

"You know that we installed cameras at Joe's house. But we also installed them at Joe's cabin, when you went to lie down," Gemma said, hating what was happening. "So we have damn-near everything recorded from the cabin, where you just came from with your so-called kidnappers. Plus, Galen and Zack were there and heard damn-near everything from outside the windows."

Rebecca turned to look at them. "This is ridiculous. You can't actually think that I would hurt Becky."

"I have no idea what you would do," Galen noted. "I don't know you, but I've seen enough to know I don't need or want to know any more about you," Galen said. "What I've heard out of your mouth is ridiculous as it is. You're not my kind of people."

She sneered. "You're male. I'm female—that makes me your kind of people. But don't worry, I don't want anything to do with you either. You're a loser."

"Absolutely," he said. "By your standards, I probably am. That makes me a winner by mine." And, with that, he looked down, smiled at Becky, and said, "It'll be okay."

She nodded and turned to look up at her mom. "What did you do?"

"I didn't do anything," her mom snapped. "Remember who you're talking to."

Chapter 15

G EMMA WINCED AT that. "Man, if I had a dollar for every time our mother said that to us ..."

"Absolutely," Rebecca said. "And I'm raising my daughter just the same way."

"Why would you do that?" Gemma asked. "You know how much she hated me."

"Of course I do," she said. "But Becky won't be like you, I won't allow it. No matter how hard you try."

"And what exactly is that? She likes animals. She likes being out in the country. What do you mean by, *not like me?*"

"She'll behave and be a good girl. She'll marry well, and she'll do her mother proud."

"Not likely," she said. "That's your agenda, not hers. She should be able to make her life as she wants it and to be happy living it," Gemma protested.

"Which is precisely why you never got along with Mom and Dad. They wanted you to be somebody."

"Like you? How's that working for you so far?" Galen asked.

She just glared and turned her back on him. Walking over to the couch, she threw herself down and said, "Now what?"

Tim chose that moment to step inside. "Well, I'm kind

of hoping that now that these two have been caught, you'll leave our people to the peace and quiet they crave," he said to Rebecca, then his gaze softened as it rested on Galen and Gemma and Becky.

With a sigh, Gemma walked over and gave him a gentle hug. "Thank you for stepping up for us," she said. "And you're right. We don't want to cause you any more trouble than we already have."

"Oh, yay," Rebecca said. "Does this mean we can finally leave Hicksville?"

Tim looked at her, then looked at Gemma. "You were so right to come here all those summers."

"I know," she said, giving him a gentle smile. "My sister would never understand because she's very much like my mother."

"And when are they leaving?" he asked, looking pointedly at the two unconscious men on the ground.

Galen gave him a ghost of a smile. "As soon as we can. I'm not sure that there aren't a few more villains in the midst of all this. I want a chance to talk to these two."

Tim nodded. "Noon?"

Galen gave him a direct nod. "Noon it is."

Tim smiled. "I'll go back and try to get some sleep," he said. "It's only three hours 'til milking time." He shook his head, headed back out, shaking his head again. "City folk."

Gemma called out behind him, "I'm sorry, Tim."

He lifted a hand, holding the rifle, and waved. "That's why you came. I'm glad we could help. Hopefully you'll stay out of trouble after this."

"I hope so too." Then she turned to look at Galen. "He was really the only source of help I knew to call when we got into trouble."

"As I keep saying," Rebecca said, "we weren't in trouble. Once again you're making something out of nothing. You're really very tiresome, Gemma."

"So you say, but I don't believe you." Galen reached down and one by one grabbed the two men and put them on the couch beside Rebecca. Both of them were still unconscious, one tilting over against Rebecca.

She bolted to her feet. "Ew! I don't want to be touched by them."

"You've had sex with both of them. What difference does it make?" Galen asked in a mocking voice.

She glared at him. "I have sex when I want to have sex, with whom I want to have sex with. But nobody's allowed to touch me if I don't want them to touch me."

"Stop that talk around Becky," Gemma demanded. Her sister obviously didn't care about that. Walking over to Becky, she said, "How about you getting some more sleep?"

Becky looked up at Gemma, and her bottom lip trembled. In a little voice, she whispered, "Did Mommy kill Daddy?"

Her mother spun and looked at her and said, "I did not kill your father. I told you that."

"And what kind of scenario makes *this* okay?" Gemma said. "That your daughter actually has to ask you that question?"

Rebecca glared at her. "I told her that we were leaving him."

"And was that before Daddy died?" Gemma asked Becky.

Her eyes welling up with tears, and her bottom lip trembling, she nodded. "Then Daddy died."

"Did you know this man who came into the house and

shot Daddy?" As she spoke, she pointed out one of the unconscious men.

Becky nodded. "He's been there lots of times."

Rebecca snapped, "Just shut up. You're too young to know what's happening here."

"At the house?"

Becky nodded.

At that, Gemma turned to look at her sister. "Seriously? You carried on an affair at home while your daughter was there?"

"She was at school. She doesn't know anything," Rebecca snarled. "Besides she's too young to understand."

"Except for when I came home from school," Becky said, "and you were in bed with him. I asked Daddy about it too."

Rebecca stared at her in horror. "You what? First rule is, you don't tell Daddy anything! How dare you?"

At that, Becky's lips trembled again.

Gemma immediately reached for her niece. "You've done nothing wrong, sweetie," she said. "Don't ever think you did." But it was obvious that the little girl was confused.

"Maybe," she said, looking back at her mom and then over at the unconscious men.

Gemma faced Rebecca. "I'll never forgive you for this," Gemma hissed, gathering Becky to her, hugging her tight.

Then Becky whispered, "Are the men dead too?"

Gemma shook her head. "No, Galen doesn't kill people," she said, "but these two are bad men, and now we have to deal with them."

Becky looked up at her. "Will he kill them then?"

"No," Gemma said, hating that this sweet little girl had gotten such a harsh view of the world. "Nobody here will kill them."

"If you give the gun to Mommy, she would."

Silence.

Galen let out a burst of laughter. It was a sad laugh, but it was either that or reach out and smack the woman for being such a horrible mother.

"Unfortunately, you're probably right," Gemma said. "But I think your mommy prefers to get other people to do her dirty work for her."

Galen looked at Gemma and motioned her and Becky toward the bedroom.

She nodded. "Come on, sweetheart. You're tired. It's been a rough night, so let's get some sleep."

"What about the men?"

"I promise Galen won't hurt them," she said.

Becky took a moment to study them all, and then she nodded. "I'm really tired. I don't like this. I want to leave now."

"It's all right. You're right to feel that way," Galen said. "Nobody should like something like this. It's bad for everybody. So get some sleep and let us deal with it. When you wake up again, we should be through the worst of it."

Becky nodded, reached up her arms, and he gave her a quick hug and a kiss on the cheek. "Go get some sleep, sweetheart."

Gemma picked up the little girl and carried her back into the bedroom. As she tucked her into bed, Becky whispered, "Will you stay?"

"Sure. I'll stay until you go to sleep," she said. She laid down on the bed beside her niece. Holding her close, she whispered, "It's going to be okay."

"No, it's not," she said. "Mommy shot Daddy, Aunt

Gemma. I saw her."

GALEN WAS CLOSE enough to the bedroom that he heard. He spun ever-so-slowly to look at Rebecca, who stared back at him in shock.

She shook her head. "No, I didn't. I didn't kill my husband."

"Yes, you did," a man from the couch said in a tired and worn-out voice.

It was the second guy Galen had knocked out, the gunman in the cabin, now conscious.

"I didn't want to do it, so you took the gun from my hand and shot him right in the forehead."

"You stupid bastard," she said. "If you would just shut up, nobody would know anything."

"Doesn't matter," he said. "The cops will be involved, and it'll be a hell of a mess now."

"No, it's not," she sneered. "You're just lying to get yourself out of trouble, and it won't work."

"Oh, it'll work," he said. "I have copies of the emails and everything about our relationship. It'll definitely work."

"Not at all," she said. "It's my word against yours."

"Yes," he said, "my word against your word." And he sneered. "What makes you think that yours is any better than ours anyway?"

At that, she realized he was pointing to the other man, still unconscious at her side.

She frowned. "You don't know anything."

"No?" he said. "I'm sure I don't. I'm sure you're full of all kinds of little tricks. I'm still trying to figure out if we were just pawns in the whole mess. I'm pretty sure we were. I just don't know who else you're dealing with above us."

"Why would I be dealing with anybody above you?" she asked. A new tone had entered her voice.

Galen looked at her and smiled. "Joe's brother, by any chance? Because this isn't him."

She looked at him, frowned, and said, "James isn't here."

"He has a big place in America, doesn't he?"

She nodded slowly. "It's really pretty," she said. "I was hoping to go over there. Make a new life for my little girl."

"I'm sure you were. All you had to do was get rid of Joe first, huh?" She lied so damn smoothly that he knew she'd been doing it all her life. And even worse, expected it to work.

"That wasn't me," she said. "That was these guys. And James was probably paying them. I didn't set this up, and Becky doesn't know what she saw."

"If you get your new lover involved in this mess," he said, "it won't bode well when it comes to building a new life for yourself."

"It doesn't matter," she said, with yet another wave of her hand. She stepped out on the front step, and he could see the sun hadn't yet risen.

"I wouldn't go out there too far by yourself," he said.

"Why not?" she said. "It's not like I'll run away without my daughter."

"You really think these guys came here alone?"

"What? You think there was somebody else?" She stared at him, her eyes huge. "I don't know anybody else who would come."

"Well, James for one."

"No, he's back in America," she protested. "Why do you keep bringing him up?"

"But is he? You're standing there in the middle of the front door to this cabin, as if somebody could shoot you. Or maybe as a signal that you need help. I don't trust you one bit," he said.

"You shouldn't," the conscious man on the couch said. "And you're right. It's all making sense now. I thought it was all pretty shitty myself, but I'm just another idiot who fell for her lies."

"What were you getting out of the deal?" Galen asked him.

"Not enough," he said. "I was supposed to get fifty thousand, if this came off without a hitch—or five thousand if there was trouble, and I just needed running money. But I'd also been having sex with her for six months, entertaining the thought in the back of my mind that maybe there was a life here for me with her too."

She snorted at that. "You were never part of the equation."

"No," he said. "Like everybody else, I was just a means to an end. Took me a while to figure it out, but I got there eventually."

"No, not even that," she said. "I needed you to take out my husband. But you were too gutless to even do that."

Galen listened with interest as she very clearly said it wasn't him who had killed her husband. Had she then? And possibly doesn't want to leave any witnesses behind? He looked over at the gunman, who nodded.

"See? Listen to her. I didn't kill him."

But the only way she'd be talking like that was if she has a surefire way of getting out of here. And immediately he got even more suspicious. Pulling out his phone, he slipped back to the side, where he was a little bit out of the way and sent a message to Zack. When there was no answer, he swore. Immediately he walked down the hallway to where Becky and Gemma were, and both were missing.

From the front step of the cabin, Rebecca laughed and laughed. "You're such an idiot," she said. "You haven't understood how this has come down right from the beginning."

"So, what will you do?" he asked. "Kill your sister and your daughter?"

"My sister, yes, and that's just for being such a bitch over this whole scenario. If she had just left me at home, none of this would have happened. But not my daughter."

"At least not today. I mean, if you've already killed your husband, plan to kill your only sister, who knows who else you might have to kill in the meantime or will have to kill later."

"Won't matter," she said, "because you won't be around to fix anything. Doesn't matter what you've heard or what you think you've heard," she said, "because you're done here."

"And if I'm not?"

"Oh, you are," she said, "and so are these two." Just then the window shattered behind him. He hit the ground running, and, by the time he got up on the other side of the cabin in the darkness, just out of the range of the window, he could see that the backs of the two thugs' heads had been blown off. And, of Rebecca, there was no sign.

Chapter 16

GEMMA STARED, FURY in her gaze as she cuddled her niece tightly in her arms. Becky was out cold. They'd knocked out the little girl, probably to still her crying or screaming. She looked at the bruising on the little girl's head, worried they may have hit her too hard. Gemma had also been hit and knocked out but woke a few minutes ago. She was tied up, whereas Becky was not.

She gently stroked Becky's hair, as that was almost the limit of her hand movement with her wrists tied up, while whispering in her ear, "Wake up, sweetheart. Wake up."

They were in the back of a station wagon, driving down what was probably the same road heading back to town that they'd been on earlier. But it was still dark out. She'd been unconscious, but it had only been for a brief time. At least she thought so. She saw no sign of morning light.

She saw just the driver and nobody else with him to look after her and Becky. So the driver wasn't expecting trouble out of the two of them. She'd love to prove him wrong. Before she had been taken and knocked out, Gemma thought she'd heard voices, and she couldn't be sure what part her sister had in this. That she was involved at all just made Gemma even angrier. She also couldn't identify the man who'd driven them away. Since she had been in the bedroom, along with Becky, it made sense that they'd been taken out the window. If only to not alert Galen and Zack. And where was Zack? She didn't know when she'd last seen him.

Had they also hurt Galen? She'd find that very unforgivable. Not that these guys would give a shit. They'd already shot how many men now? And had they killed their own thugs?

She'd heard sounds of gunfire behind them as they'd left, and her stomach cramped to think who'd taken a bullet. It was just disturbing to think that any of this was going on at all. She'd come to realize that it didn't matter what kind of excuses she made, her sister was just rotten to the core. It didn't make sense that she would continue with this—unless she had really killed Joe. And Gemma had to believe Becky on that one. So, if Rebecca killed Joe, she would have to pay for that crime. So Rebecca could still be hoping to get out of that consequence somehow. The fact that Becky had seen her mother shoot her father was another very troubling detail. Rebecca kept denying it, but apparently she had been Joe's killer. According to Becky. And according to the guy at the cabin.

If Gemma still had her phone, she could check the conversation she'd recorded secretly while they'd been talking. But she had no way to know if it had recorded properly. If nothing else it would be evidence for a trial. Although she couldn't imagine having to be a witness against her own sister. Poor Becky. Gemma couldn't feel the phone in her pocket, but that didn't mean it wasn't there.

Just then Becky's eyes drifted open and then closed again.

"Becky, wake up," she whispered gently. "Please, honey. We're in trouble."

Becky's eyes opened, but her gaze was unfocused. "Auntie Gemma?"

"Yes, it's me. I need you to listen carefully. We've been kidnapped, so you need to keep your voice very low."

Becky's eyes focused on her aunt's face, and she looked around in shock.

But Gemma was waiting for that and held her firmly against her. "You can't sit up because somebody is driving the vehicle. We don't want him to know we're awake, okay?" The car radio was on and producing just enough volume that she was hoping he couldn't hear their whispers.

Becky looked at her with huge brown eyes swimming with fear.

Gemma nodded gently. "We were taken from the cabin. They hit you over the head. I'm so sorry, Becky, that I couldn't stop them from hurting you. They hit me too," she said, "but you were out for much longer." Gemma reached up her hands, to show her that she was tied up, then gently stroked Becky's hair. In turn, Becky stroked Gemma's face.

"Are you okay?" she whispered.

"My head hurts, but I'm okay." Gemma smiled gently. "I am, sweetie. I just don't know how badly hurt you are."

"I'm okay. Where are we going?" Becky whispered hoarsely. She laid her head down on Gemma's chest, her arms wrapped around her.

Becky was just close enough that Gemma could kiss her forehead. "I don't know, sweetheart, but we have to be ready."

"I don't want to be ready," the little girl whispered. "I'm scared. I just want to go home. I want Daddy."

Gemma's heart broke at that. Needing her niece to focus on something, she asked, "Can you see if you can untie my hands?"

The little girl tried to sit up, but Gemma held her close. "We can't have you rise above the seat," she said. "We're in the back. They just threw us inside, and, if we go higher than the level of the seats, they'll see us." She held up her hands again.

Becky twisted around and took a look, then set to work trying to untie them.

It was a surprise when she managed to get it undone. But, as soon as her hands were untied, Gemma snatched the little girl, laid her down, and whispered, "Can you work on my feet?"

The valiant little girl awkwardly bent over and twisted around and worked on untying her feet. Gemma at least had shoes on, whereas Becky was still in her nightclothes, and her feet were bare. Blankets were wrapped around them, so they had just been snatched up as they were, but it would have taken two men to do that. No way would somebody make a second trip. Becky managed to get Gemma's feet untied, and the vehicle just kept going down the road through the night.

Gemma looked at her options. Finding her phone in her pocket, she smiled and sent a text. With her phone on mute, she checked her battery power. It was at 67 percent. She had to keep an eye on that. Then she sent Galen a second text, giving him the update that they were free but in a vehicle being driven by a single person and that both had been snatched out of the bedroom. Probably by two men. That she may have a recording of her sister and her goons. She was so relieved when she got a response a few moments later.

Leave your phone on. Will track you.

She smiled, returned her phone to her pocket, then laid back down again, a little more comfortable. She grabbed

Becky and held her close, whispering, "Galen is coming for us."

Becky whispered back, "Good. I like him." And then, in her tiny voice, she asked, "Is he coming now?"

"Yes. He's coming now, but it'll take him a bit." She held her close and whispered, "Stay positive, honey."

"Did my mommy do this?"

"I don't know how much of this is her doing," Gemma replied, her heart breaking for the horror her niece had been through, "but she's involved to a certain extent."

"I didn't want to think my mommy was bad."

"Bad is a hard thing to say," she said. "You know your mommy loves you."

"But she loved Daddy, and she shot him."

"Are you sure you saw that?"

She nodded. "I did, but she said I was dreaming."

"Of course." That explained the little girl's confusion and the uncertainty in her statements. And so typical of her sister. Rebecca had always been great at twisting things around and making you wonder if you'd actually heard what you thought you'd heard. "Unfortunately those tricks won't save her now," she said.

"What'll happen to me then?" Becky questioned sincerely.

"Nothing. You aren't bad, and you didn't have anything to do with this," she said.

"But she's my mom. If she's bad, am I bad?"

Gemma winced at that because a lot of people certainly believed that the sins of the parents were handed down to the children, and she didn't want Becky thinking that she had inherited those bad things because of her mom.

"I don't think that at all," she said. "You are a beautiful

little girl, and your heart is good."

"I don't like hurting people," she said.

"And you don't like being hurt either, do you?"

Becky shook her head. "No."

"Unfortunately you know a lot about what happened."

"But I don't want to know," she said. Her voice hardened. "I don't want to have to tell people what she did."

"Well, you'll have to tell somebody," she said. She looked up at her and said, "I could record it."

"Tape it," she whispered. "Then I don't have to tell anyone." Wincing at that because she also knew her battery was an issue, she pulled out her phone, turned it on Record, and said, "Go ahead."

"I watched my mommy shoot my daddy," she said. "Then he fell down and landed at the bottom of the stairs. She was fighting with another man in the living room, and they were talking about the man killing Daddy first. This man had been to my mommy's bed many times. I saw him there and other men too."

"Do you know who your uncle is?"

"Yes. His name is James. She was sleeping with James too. But I think there was somebody else."

It broke Gemma's heart to hear her little niece say this stuff. "Did your mom treat you okay?"

"When she wasn't yelling at me, yes. She said we had to look after ourselves, or nobody else would."

"You know that's wrong, right? Because I will always look after you," she said.

"Good," she said, "because I think I'm a bad person now."

"And that's not true," she said. "You're not. Did you ever hear your mommy make plans for a new life?" And her heart broke a little more when Becky nodded. "You have to say yes or no, sweetheart."

"Yes," she said. "We were moving to the US. And we'd have a big house with a swimming pool. I really want the swimming pool." Her voice turned sad. "I guess there's no swimming pool now, is there?"

Inside, Gemma wondered what the chances were that she could find a place with a pool just for the little girl because she had no doubt that she would end up being the one who raised her now. "I don't know about that," she said. "That's not today's issue."

Becky nodded. "Am I going to jail?"

"No," she said, "you didn't do anything wrong."

"But I didn't tell the police what she did to Daddy. I lied."

There was a moment of silence while Gemma looked for the right answer. "And why did you lie?"

"Mommy said to because she would get in trouble. Then she kept telling me that I didn't see what I saw, that people wouldn't believe me, and that I'd get into trouble for lying."

"So she told you one thing, then told you something different, and then something different again?"

Becky hesitated and then whispered, "Yes."

"She's good at that, isn't she?"

"She's very good at that."

At that point, she turned off the recorder. "If you can sleep," she said, "do it. I don't know how far of a drive we'll have, but we'll need our rest."

"What about you?" she asked.

"I'll just stay here and keep you safe."

"You need rest too. When will Galen come?" Becky whispered as she snuggled in closer.

"I trust that Galen's on his way," she said. "You should too."

"Is Zack okay?" she asked.

"You tell me," she said. "Have you ever heard anything about Zack?"

"Only that Mom said he's an idiot, and she only wanted him around for as long as he was useful."

"I forgot how difficult your mother could be. Do you like Zack?"

"I like him," she said. "He's nicer than the others."

"I think Zack's okay," Gemma said, deliberately not asking about the others.

"I don't think Mom was sleeping with him," she said.

"Not for a long time anyway," she said. "It was before your daddy."

"Oh." She stopped and then whispered, "It's not right to sleep with men like that, is it?"

She didn't have a clue how much her little niece understood about sex and the term "sleeping with men." She shrugged and held her close. "Let's try not to judge. Your mom is who she is."

"Is she going to jail?"

Gemma winced at that. "It's possible, yes." Because, of course, she should go to jail if she had killed Joe. He had been a good man. He didn't deserve to have the woman he absolutely adored turn on him.

But then that was Rebecca's specialty. To make men fall in love with her, then turn that love into something so dark and so nasty that they were twisted up and messed up forever afterward.

She was grateful Zack appeared to have gotten out of the cycle. "We'll just wait and see."

"If I don't have to go to jail with Mom, can I stay with you?"

Gemma took the opportunity to hold her as close as she could and whispered against her hair, "Always." And, with that, Becky snuggled in deep and relaxed.

"WE HAVE TO find them," Galen said. Zack was running GPS from the passenger side, while Galen pushed the vehicle as fast as he could, the headlights off to hide them from their prey, so he was driving in the dark on the rough unlit road. Unfortunately they weren't gaining. "They can't be too far ahead, but I see no sign of them."

"Well, they are. We've also got Tim to thank for taking care of those bodies too," he said.

"That Tim guy's very interesting."

"As long as he does his job, I don't care," Zack said. "He's been good to Gemma."

"They don't want cops on the property."

"I know. I think they'll move the bodies into the vehicle and move them somewhere else."

Galen thought about it and then said, "Send him a text and tell him to take them to Joe's cabin. That will at least put them in another location, tying them all to Joe's murder investigation. Or at least to have the local cops open up an investigation into Joe's murder."

"Will do."

Galen hated to think that both Becky and Gemma were now missing. The real kidnappers might keep Becky safe, but Galen was pretty sure Gemma would get tossed into a ditch somewhere. Apparently the sanctity of life didn't matter to anybody in that group. "I also think that bloody bitch

Rebecca got away clean too. Need to track her down and fast."

"I'm not surprised," Zack said. "She's a survivor, always has been."

"You should have shot her years ago."

Zack snorted. "Believe me. I was tempted."

"I'm not at all surprised." Up ahead of them, he thought he saw something go around a corner. "That can't be them ahead of us."

"Well, it's somebody, but it's not Gemma."

"Interesting. Maybe it's our mystery shooter and Rebecca."

"If that's the case, go faster," Zack said, his voice harsh. "I'd like to see that bitch one more time."

"She's in this up to her neck."

"I see that. Believe me. Nothing's quite so plain as the light of day afterward."

It was a bit cryptic, but Galen was pretty sure Zack was more or less saying that he now saw Rebecca for what she really was. Galen picked up a little bit of speed, swinging wide around a corner, and it shot him a little bit farther ahead.

He could see the vehicle ahead, and it's almost as if they saw him behind them and were trying desperately to get away from Galen and Zack. But the driver was pushing his vehicle as fast as he could go. But then, so were they. The driver was also still running in the dark, but now Galen was clearly gaining on them.

"You've got the advantage of being in their tailwind," Zack said.

"If I can just get close enough," he said, "I'll turn on my headlights, so we can see who it is."

"I'm pretty damn sure I know who."

"Has Levi got satellite on it?"

"Stone's tracking them. He's also got a location for Gemma. About ten miles away."

"Interesting. Wonder where they're going."

Zack said, "Rebecca could be as amiable as she wanted to be, but she's always thinking in the background."

"She's devious and out of control," Galen bit off. Zack didn't say anything. Which was probably a damn good thing. "As long as you've not got anything to do with her at this point," he said.

"I've told you time and time again, I don't."

"I hear you, but, when somebody like that gets their claws into you—"

"That's not me," Zack snorted. "Not any longer."

"Good," he said, and he left it at that.

He was gaining a little bit at a time, and, when Galen thought he was close enough, he put on his high beams and shone them right into the back of the vehicle. Definitely two heads, one female on the side. The other vehicle hit the brakes momentarily, probably blinded by Galen's high beams. And it was just enough for Galen to catch up that little bit. And now they had a license plate.

Zack quickly reeled it off to Levi's group. It came back as a rental. "Interesting," Zack said. "We didn't see that sticker before. They're tracking down who rented it." After a short pause, Zack added, "It came back to the company owned by James."

"So now we have Joe's brother renting a vehicle over here. Do we know if he's here or not?"

"Checking now. Don't forget. It could be anyone from the brewery, but, from what we know, James is the most likely suspect."

When Zack's phone buzzed back and forth, it was all Galen could do not to ask questions with every exchange. But it was what it was.

Finally Zack said, "James entered Switzerland fourteen hours ago, confirmed. He's traveling with his son. Supposedly heading to a property in Bern. Reason given was for a holiday, not business."

"And still could have hopped a plane under an alias and been in Germany in one hour. So he could have been here for all this latest chaos, but he wasn't in the country for Joe's murder."

"Do you really have any doubt who killed Joe?"

"Nope. Not after Becky said she saw it."

"That's got to be tough, to see your mother shoot your father," Zack said.

"Yeah," he said. "None of this has been easy on her. It makes no sense, and she'll have trouble sorting it all out in her mind afterward."

"Sure enough. But she's a great kid. She's resilient."

Just then the vehicle ahead slowed down. Galen watched as they appeared to lose power all at once. The vehicle pulled off to the side. "Interesting twist. What the hell?"

"It's almost like they ran out of gas," Zack said, with a smug tone.

Galen looked at him. "Did you puncture the gas tank?"

"Well, I tried, but I didn't get much chance," he said. "I did put some stuff in the gas tank though, but that can take a long time to sift through."

"Looks like it might have finally worked."

"Now we'll have to watch it," he said, "because we're the sitting ducks."

"Yes, we can expect them to be armed and dangerous." Galen pulled up behind them, keeping a good distance, and Zack immediately got out and ducked below his open door. No sign of life was in the vehicle stopped in front of them. Zack got back into the passenger's side. "Keep close."

Galen drove slowly closer, keeping himself hunched down behind the dash, so he could just barely see, and he ran his vehicle right into theirs.

"What the hell will that do?" he heard Zack say.

Galen kept driving forward, kept pushing the other truck into the ditch and off to the side, slamming into a tree at the bottom. As soon as that happened, Galen hopped out, his vehicle now at the top of the ditch, the engine still running, and the emergency brake on. Both of the guys jumped down to the vehicle below. Galen held his gun against the open window to see one man swearing and cussing at him, blood gushing from a head wound. On the other side was Rebecca, screaming obscenities at both of them, but she also looked banged up.

Galen found it hard to be sympathetic. "The vehicle isn't badly damaged," he said. "I'm surprised she didn't run, leaving you holding the bag."

"I have a gun," the older man said, pulling up his other hand, pointing the gun at Galen.

"Yeah? So do I," Galen said with a laugh. "So what do I care. What will you do about it?"

"This," he snapped. And pointed it at Galen, his finger pulling back to fire.

Galen was faster and slammed the gun into the man's wrist, knocking the gun from his hand. He screamed at the same time Galen opened the door and pulled him out, shoving him to the ground, holding the gun to his head. On the other side, Rebecca smashed Zack on the side of his head over and over as she fought with him. Zack managed to bring the screaming, outraged woman over to the side of the vehicle. Galen stood up and told Zack to duck. As Zack leaned his head back as far as he could, Galen reached out and smacked Rebecca hard on the side of the head. She went limp and sagged to the ground. He turned to look at Zack and said, "If you can't handle her, I will."

"I got this," Zack said, swearing. "I'm just not used to hitting women."

"You shouldn't ever be used to hitting women," Galen said. "But, when the time comes, you have to be ready to do whatever needs to be done with the likes of Rebecca." With her now secured and on the ground, Galen took a look at the stranger's wrist. It was injured but not too badly. Although it was bleeding a decent amount. He ripped off a piece of the stranger's T-shirt and bound his wound up tight. "Hold on to that to stop the bleeding."

The driver clamped his hand down tight.

Galen sat back and studied the stranger. The cloud cover had added a dark heaviness to the night. He couldn't see the driver's face clearly at all. "Are you the one who just shot two men?"

The older male just glared at him.

Galen held up his cell phone and, using a flashlight app, checked the driver's face and whistled. "Look at that. We've got James here and now in Germany." At the look of surprise on the driver's face, Galen nodded. "Did you really think we don't have a full idea of what the hell is going on here?"

"Nobody could," he said. "It's bloody useless doing anything with her."

"So do you know her well?" he asked. "You shouldn't

have gotten involved in the first place."

The older man nodded slowly. "That's the truth, isn't it?"

"Screwing your brother's wife is never cool," he said. "Especially when you end up killing him to get the unfaithful wife for yourself.

The older man just glared at him.

"Are you saying that's not what happened?"

"We were both dating her at the same time," he said. "I'm a lot older than Joe. I guess she figured he was a better bet."

"Maybe not," Galen said. "I think she just likes to play the left against the right. Have you kept seeing her all these years?"

The old man groaned and then nodded slowly.

"Well, you'll have a lot of years in jail to sit there and think about the choices you made in your life."

"Maybe not," he said. "We're not out of this yet."

"Sure you are," Galen said. "We've already sent photos through satellite to our headquarters. They've contacted the police. Believe me. We'll be adding kidnapping and murder charges, so good luck with that."

"I didn't kill anybody," he said. "Certainly not my brother."

"You killed Rebecca's two goons back at the cabin. Maybe you didn't kill your brother, but you ordered the killing, and that'll go on you just the same."

"No. I didn't kill anyone. And I didn't order any killing at all," he protested. "I just responded to a SOS from Rebecca, saying she was in deep trouble and needed me."

At that, Galen sat back on his heels, looked at her, and gave a sharp laugh. "You know what? That just might work.

Because it will be—at least partially—the truth."

"It's more than partially the truth," he said. "Unfortunately, just like my brother, I've been hooked on her ever since the beginning."

Galen raised an eyebrow, looked at Zack, who stared at the old man in disgust. "See Zack? Not just you," he said.

Zack shot him a hard look. "At least I've been away from her shit show for the last eight years," he said.

"And I thought it was just Joe and I," James said sadly. "I don't even know why I'm here. I'm old enough to know better. Really."

"To rescue her. Remember? But then again, she had already killed Joe."

He looked at him in horror. "She killed my brother?"

"Of course, but I'm sure she told you somebody else did it."

"Absolutely she did. She said it was a botched burglary attempt."

"Of course," Galen said. "Except for the fact that she was seen, by two eyewitnesses. And by the hired gun's statement alone, when he balked and didn't want to shoot Joe, she grabbed the gun and shot Joe herself."

The old man just stared at him in shock.

"And if you don't believe me, James," he said, "maybe you'll believe your niece, since Becky saw the whole thing."

"My daughter saw it?"

"*Your* daughter?" Galen shook his head at that. "I hope you've had a DNA test done over that because Joe was positive she was his, and I know a couple other guys were at play around the same time. Becky could be anyone's daughter at this point. But, back to the murder issue, yes, young Becky saw her mother shoot her father," he said. "And believe me. She's pretty torn up about it. Because her mother also kept lying, saying she didn't do it and that Becky obviously didn't see what she thought she saw."

"Yeah, that's Rebecca," James said, looking down at the woman, still unconscious. "I don't have a clue what hold this Lolita has on me, and every other man around her, but it's a damn destructive one."

"Well, if you hadn't killed her two goons, you might be able to rebuild a life for yourself at some point in time, but I wouldn't count on it."

"Is that even possible?" he asked, filled with remorse. "I feel like an old fool." He shook his head and added, "But I swear that I didn't shoot anybody."

"Like I said, it depends on if you had anything to do with the killing. If you did, well, no, you can't rebuild your life. If you didn't kill anybody, I'd give it a maybe. She, on the other hand, is going to jail for murdering her husband."

Just then another vehicle slowed down on the side of the road above them. Zack immediately disappeared into the trees, and Galen whispered down at James, "I wouldn't trust anybody, if I were you, so keep your mouth shut." And, with that, he melted into the background. The vehicle pulled up to the side and called out, "Hey, Dad, is that you?"

"Yeah, it is," he said. "Victor, is that you?"

"Yeah. Hey, Dad. Are you okay?"

Galen looked on, in absolute shock and horror, as out came a strapping young man from a large station wagon. He scrambled down the loose bank to where his father sat on the ground. "What the hell happened to you?"

"She happened," he said, nodding toward Rebecca, still unconscious on the ground.

"Oh, my God. Is she okay?" he asked softly, as he quickly moved to her side. "How could this happen? Poor baby. Especially after what those assholes did to her ..."

Even Galen could hear the absolute love-swept tone in his voice. With his heart sinking, he realized that yet another player was in this game.

Father stared at son. "Did you shoot anybody over this?" James asked hesitantly, his voice thick and sad.

"Hell no. Well, not anybody who counted. ... The two men who kidnapped her are out of the way, at least. Still some cleaning up to do. Like that damn woman involved in this mess. To think she was trying to take Rebecca's child." He shook his head and, in an almost reverent voice, whispered, "My God, what this angel has been through ..."

That damn woman? Was Victor talking about Gemma? It sounded like it, but Galen knew she hadn't had anything to do with this mess.

"Yeah? What is it that she's been through?" James asked.

Galen was *not* liking this turn of events.

"Those guys kidnapped her," he said with such anger in his voice that the others stopped to stare at him. "I had to save her. Jesus, she's been through so much."

"Yeah, she has," James said, as he stared at his son in shock. "More than you know."

"I got worried, so turned around to make sure you two were okay. Obviously my instincts were correct." He dropped down, grabbing Rebecca's hand. "How did you end up down here?" Victor asked, as he studied the unconscious woman. "How badly hurt is she?"

"Not," James said.

Galen quietly shifted his position, in case things went south quickly. That Victor was acting as he was, gave Galen yet another ugly suspicion into a new Rebecca victim. Galen switched his gaze to the vehicle sitting on the road above them. Were Gemma and Becky in his vehicle?

"It's a long story," James said, sadly studying his son's face with an odd look, as if finally seeing the same thing.

"We came to rescue her," Victor said.

"We came because she called out for help, yes," he said. "I don't know that she actually needed a rescue though."

"Don't you start with me now," Victor said, getting angry. He straightened up. "I told you how important she is to me."

James gave a mocking self-depraving laugh. "No. No, you really didn't. You were really agitated about coming to help her, and, as that suited my purpose, I was on board from the beginning," he said. "However, the one thing I never had a chance to tell you was how important she was to me too."

Ooops.

A long awkward silence followed as father and son stared at each other.

Now was a really good time to step forward and put a stop to this. With Zack coming up on the one side, Galen came up on the other, his gun out. "And where's Rebecca's daughter," Galen asked. "Not to mention *the bitch* you thought was trying to take her away."

Victor froze, them palmed his own gun. "So not innocent bystanders? If you guys had anything to do with kidnapping Rebecca," he said, "I'll make sure you pay."

"Son, you don't understand," Galen said, as he stepped forward, his gun in his hand but his eyes watching the younger man's trigger finger like a hawk. "That woman is not who you think she is."

"The hell she isn't," he said. "She's my lover, and she'll

be my wife."

Galen could feel the sudden change in Zack's awareness at the same time that James laughed brokenly.

"Oh, my God," James said, "she really did it."

"She really did what?" Victor asked, looking down at his father.

"She's really been sleeping with the both of us. While she was married to my brother at the same time!" His laughter turned almost hysterical. Part of it was pain, and part of it was the horrible realization of what a fool he had been. Just then, a new element entered the situation.

From up on the roadside, a small voice called out. "Mommy?"

At that moment, Galen realized that Becky and hopefully Gemma were in that station wagon up top. The stakes had never been higher.

Chapter 17

Gemma had tried to hush Becky, but, once they'd heard the men talking and understood the gist of the conversation, they realized that Rebecca had to be there too.

Becky rolled over the back seat before Gemma could stop her and had the door open. She reached for Becky, just missing her before the little girl bolted from the vehicle. Gemma wasn't far behind and caught up to her quickly.

Now the two of them stood at the top of the hill, and she hung on to Becky tightly. Gemma looked down into the ditch to see two men she knew and two she didn't. And, of course, her sister lying there, obviously unconscious.

She called out to Galen, "Is she—"

"She's just knocked out. This is James, Joe's brother. Your driver was Victor, his son. Both of them have been sleeping with your sister."

Gemma wanted to throw up, disgusted by the way her sister had played them all and had ripped yet another family apart. She shook her head. "She wouldn't have thought a thing of it, I'm afraid," she said. And there was just so much sadness in her heart that she knew it was evident in her own voice. "I'm so sorry, James."

He just looked at her and nodded slowly. "I'm an old fool."

"Tell me that you're lying. That you aren't sleeping with

my girlfriend," Victor said, staring his father in horror. "That's disgusting."

Gemma winced, looked at him, and asked, "How old are you?"

"I'm twenty-one. Why?"

"Yeah, and how long you been sleeping with my sister?" she said.

He shrugged. "About three years. Why?"

"Well, she's been sleeping with your father for at least eight."

Victor stared at the old man, then back at her, lifting the handgun to point in her direction.

Galen shuddered. "No," he said, "no more of that."

Victor just snorted and said, "You're not stopping me. But I'm not standing here and listening to her lies."

"Of course not," Rebecca said. "Why would you even listen to Gemma. You can ask me yourself."

He turned around and everyone could see that Rebecca was slowly waking up, now sitting up on the ground, looking around at what was going on. She turned to Victor. "Just shoot them," she said, "now already."

He stared at her in confusion.

"These are the men who kidnapped me," she said with wave to Galen and Zack.

"That is a lie," Becky called out. "Galen is a good man. And she shot Daddy. I saw her."

Victor stiffened, stared at the little girl in shock, then looked back at Rebecca and asked, "What's going on here?"

"You were duped, just as I was duped," James said tiredly.

By now James's voice was getting faint, and Gemma could see the loss of blood was affecting him. He held up his hand, she guessed to stop the blood flow from his wrist wound. She figured that had probably come from Galen. But then again, maybe his own son had shot him.

As James kept talking, Victor shook his head. "No." Victor looked down at Rebecca. "You weren't sleeping with my dad, were you?"

"Of course not," she said, her face twisting in a grimace. "He's far too old."

Instantly Victor nodded and smiled. "Of course. Of course she wouldn't."

"She's lying," Gemma said. "Ask Becky."

Becky looked at the young man. "I saw him in bed with her. Yes."

"That's disgusting. You don't understand anything. You're just a child," he said, and he pointed the gun at the little girl.

"Is that who you are?" his father said to Victor. "A little girl says something you don't like, and you plan to kill her? How does that even begin to make sense of who you are as a man?"

"Well, he isn't a man though, is he?" Gemma said with a tired sigh. "He's just another one of Rebecca's conquests."

"Another?" Victor asked.

"She's had dozens over the last ten years," Gemma said. She had deliberately drawn the attention to herself, waving her hands and pointing around, so that Galen and Zack could make a move. She continued, "As her sister, I've watched her forever playing these games, pitting man against man, over and over again. It's not much fun seeing all the men fall like dominoes around her, filled with her lies and her cheating ways. Joe was a good man. He didn't deserve to have his wife cheat with his own brother and his own nephew. And she was trying to raise her daughter to be the same way."

Becky looked up and said, "But I'm not like her. I don't want anything to do with her. She shot Daddy."

At that, Galen pounced on Victor. The gun went off but fired harmlessly into the ditch. He kicked it out of Victor's hand. With one strong uppercut, he knocked out the young man, who fell beside his father. James looked down at his son and whispered, "What a sad day."

"The sad day," Gemma said to him quietly, "is the day that you first slept with your brother's wife."

He looked up at her, and she could see the truth in his eyes as he slowly nodded. "And apparently that's a mistake I'll pay for forever."

"You *and* your son," she said. "And unfortunately, Becky too." She looked from father to son. "And which one of you lowlifes hit this child?"

Once Galen had the young man restrained and their weapons secured, he climbed the ditch and wrapped her up in his arms. She hugged him tight. "It's over now," he said. "I'm so sorry you and Becky were snatched out of that cabin."

Nodding, she smiled. "Oh, but Becky was brave and did a great job of getting me untied."

He crouched in front of her. "Now that was an awesome job. Thanks for helping Gemma."

She beamed and smiled up at him. "Thank you," she said. "I wanted to help."

"You were a big help," he said. He chuckled when she threw her arms around him. He picked her up and held her close. "Soon this will just be a bad memory."

She looked at him solemnly. "I won't see my mommy

again, will I?"

"She'll spend a lot of time in jail," he said. "But that doesn't mean you won't be able to see her."

"Or not." Her hard voice came from down below. And there was Rebecca, holding a gun on Zack. "You guys all just move away from that vehicle, and Zack will drive me a long way away. We'll have nothing to do with each other, and I'll be able to live some kind of a life. I am not going to jail. That would kill me."

Becky looked at her and trembled. "But then we won't see each other. If you go to jail, I can see you."

"Nope. We won't see each other. You've already made a choice to be more like Gemma," she said in disgust. "There's no hope for you anymore." Her voice was cruel and cutting and brought tears to her daughter's eyes.

Immediately Gemma stepped forward. "That's not true," she said. "She's already a way better person than you ever were."

"Oh, you're such a goody-goody," she said. "Just shut up for once, won't you."

"Put the gun down," Galen said. "You've got no reason to hurt Zack."

"Of course not," she said. "Zack was my lover once. He's also the only one I couldn't manage to keep on a string." She glared at him. "Why the hell was that?"

"It took me a while," he said, "but eventually I did see through the sparkly veneer to the poison beneath."

With a quick and seamless move, he reached up, smacked her hard across the side of her face, then grabbed her wrist and took the gun from her hand. While she stood there sputtering, he pulled her arms behind her, secured her, and sat her down beside James. "You're going to jail, whether you like it or not."

Glaring at him, she screamed obscenities.

Finally James looked at her and said, "Shut the fuck up."

Stunned, she collapsed against the vehicle, weeping.

Zack looked at Galen. "If there wasn't a cure before, this has been one hell of a good cure now."

"You were already pretty free and clear," he said. "That just put an end to all the last little bits and pieces."

"Can we get some bloody help now?" James called out. "I'm not climbing up on my own. My wrist is killing me." He chuckled, though his mirth was short-lived because another vehicle came up the road. He waited for it to pull by, but it slowed.

Galen was tense until he realized who it was. Tim hopped out and looked over the group. Gemma walked over to him.

"Do you guys always leave a trail like this?" Tim asked.

"Thanks for coming," she said. "And I promise this is all of them."

He nodded and said, "Well, I'm bringing in the cops too," he said to the group as a whole. "I sure as hell don't want them at my place very long." He looked back at her and said, "You are welcome to visit again, but you can leave the rest of them behind."

With a smile, she walked closer and gave Tim a hug.

"You can bring Becky, though."

Galen watched as the two embraced gently. An obvious affection and respect were there. He heard an exchange between them but didn't know exactly what was said. Still, he was grateful their relationship would survive this violent intrusion into Tim's peaceful oasis.

It took another forty minutes for the cops to show up,

and, when they did, all kinds of hell broke loose. It took time for the statements and the ambulances. By the time the prisoners were taken away, the cops followed the rest of them back to the cabins to look for forensic evidence. One team broke away to investigate Joe's cabin.

By the time everything was cleared away, it was just Galen, Zack, Gemma, and Becky. The only reason Becky was still with Gemma was because Gemma had said that she was the child's guardian.

As they stood outside, tired and exhausted, Galen looked at the receding taillights of the law enforcement vehicles. Then turned to Gemma. "You'll look after her?" Galen asked.

She looked at him steadily, and he knew that she would.

He smiled and nodded. "Then I know she'll be okay."

She gave him a bright smile. "Thanks for the vote of confidence. It's one thing to be an aunt but another thing altogether being a parent."

"Particularly the parent of a little girl who has been through a lot of trauma," Zack said. He walked over and smacked Galen on the shoulder. "Man, you sure leave a lot of bodies behind."

"Not me," Galen said. "Generally I'm a neat and tidy guy."

Tim joined them, obviously happy the place was clearing out. He looked down at the little girl and Gemma. "So now what?" he asked Gemma.

She smiled at Tim and said, "Well, now that the chaos is over, would you allow us to stay for a day or two to recover?"

He considered her for a long moment, studied the others, and finally spoke. "No more fights? No more weapons? No more shootings?" They all nodded. "Fine," he said. "Two more days, that's what I'll agree to." He looked down at the little girl and reached out a hand. "Did you know we've got kittens?"

Her eyes lit up. "Baby kittens?"

"Yes. Born just this morning, if you want to come see them."

She immediately put her hand into his.

He looked at them. "Enjoy your time."

"Will do."

Zack laughed and said, "Well, I'm pretty sure what that meant," he said. "I'll go get some rest. I'll take the cabin with the bloodstains. You guys take the other one." He walked into the little cabin where Gemma had been earlier.

Galen looked at her. "Do you want to lie down? You must be exhausted."

"I'm tired, wound up, frustrated, angry, devastated, sad, and, at the same time, incredibly overjoyed that it's over."

He walked her into the other cabin and right back to the bedroom in the rear.

"What about here?" he asked. "Can you rest here?"

She smiled, wrapped her arms around his neck, and said, "You really don't want to waste the time that we've been given by sleeping, do you?"

He looked around and said, "Was that deliberate?"

She chuckled. "For a smart guy, you're pretty obtuse sometimes."

"Seriously?"

She reached up, put her lips softly against his, and whispered, "Seriously." She knew he was shocked, but she'd understood Zack's meaning and knew that Tim was giving them time alone. She would take whatever time alone she could get, now that she'd have a little one with her all the time.

When she kissed him, she wasn't kissing him to make the best use of their time but to let him know that she cared. As she finally pulled back, she hooked her arms around his neck. "Did I say thank you?"

He wrapped his arms around her and tucked her up close. "No need," he whispered. "I came as backup to Zack, and apparently we were both your backup. Though I have to admit that you did a pretty damn good job right from the beginning." He reached out and kissed her again. "I came over expecting to investigate some problem in the brewery, not to find you'd already got wind of something dangerous and had spirited away your sister and niece."

"Too bad I wasn't willing to see what my sister was truly like."

"Not sure anyone could have seen that," he whispered, holding her close.

"It'll be a mess to clean up."

"Yes, it will. More so to shield Becky from the worst of it."

She nodded. "I'll move back to the USA too," she said. "Becky needs a new home to make new memories, while we build her a whole new life. She wants a pool. Maybe I can find a house with a pool. And I'll shift my job, so I can stay home and can work remotely, now that I have her full-time."

"I agree with that," he said. "Perfect."

"And maybe you'd like to consider being part of her life going forward?"

"I would be honored," he said gently.

She knew that he meant it. "And maybe part of mine?" she whispered, gently rubbing her nose against his.

"I am so looking forward to that," he said with a chuckle. His hands slid up under Gemma's shirt, coming to rest against her ribs.

"I'm not the Lolita my sister is," she said half hesitantly.

His eyebrows shot up. "Thank God for that," he whispered fervently. "I'd much rather have someone like you in my life over someone like her. Please, don't ever think you're less than her. You are so much more—and in all the ways that matter."

She smiled, tightening her arms around his neck. "Thank you for that."

"Don't thank me," he said. "If we all learned anything this weekend, it's the difference between the two of you. You are somebody to spend the rest of my life with," he said. "I wouldn't even give someone like Rebecca the time of day."

Gemma pulled him closer and kissed him passionately. She poured everything she had within her into it, including all the insecurities her mother and sister had filled her with. But his response left her with no doubt, as he held her close. Before she was aware of it, she was stretched out on the bed. Her shirt was off; her jeans were off, and she was there in nothing but tiny panties. She looked down and back up at him in surprise. "Wow, are you ever smooth."

"No," he corrected gently. "Just needy. I've wanted you since I first met you. I might be slow on the uptake, but now that I understand what we have between us, I'm not letting you go."

He joined her on the bed, his arms careful and gentle, yet the look in his eyes made her feel so beautiful. It was as if he'd never even seen her sister. She smiled and stroked her finger across his lips. "I love that look in your eyes."

His gaze moved slowly down her long, lean body, his fingers trailing right after it. He looked up at her words, then smiled. "The look in my gaze is one of disbelief," he said with passion. "Because you are stunning. Absolutely gorgeous." He leaned over, his tongue flicking across her collarbone, up her neck to her chin. Then he dropped kisses along her bottom lip. His fingers slid underneath her head, and she arched into them. He trailed kisses down her neck, then across the plump top of her breast, and suckled gently. She twisted and moaned in his arms. He repeated the action on the other side, his hands holding her firm while he explored the valley between them.

"That feels so damn good," she whispered.

"It's supposed to," he said. "But it's supposed to feel good for you, not just a case of seduction with a purpose. This is supposed to be because we want and need each other."

She smiled and realized it was another reference to her sister and her manipulations. "The only reason I want to be here is because I want to be with you. But if you're going to tease me," she whispered, "you'll have to do it fast, because I'm not waiting."

He chuckled. "What will you do about it then?"

She flipped him over in a move that had him lying here, gasping in surprise, but he was already completely nude, and his erection stood tall and proud.

"Well, that was easy," she said. "So I'll take my turn." She lowered her head and kissed him gently on the lips, then let her hand stroke his heavily muscled body, the scars each receiving kisses and strokes of concern as she slowly worked her way down his body, completely ignoring his groans and attempts to grab her. She stroked his thighs and his calves, even his toes, tickling them until he was laughing.

When she covered his erection with both hands, he

groaned, his hips coming off the bed. "You can't do that," he whispered.

"Oh, I understand," she said, her voice thick, "because I feel the same way." She slowly crawled up his body again, so she was astride him, and, with his hands at her hips for support, she lowered herself on his shaft, both of them moaning in joy as they came together. When she was fully seated, she looked down at him and said, "You know one of the things that I learned to do when I was here years ago?"

His gaze unfocused, he stared up at her. "No, what was that?"

She smiled. "I learned to ride."

And ever-so-slowly she leaned forward and started to rise and fall. Slowing at first, then faster, when she finally took them over the edge, sharing the fall together. Something was so damn special about this. It wasn't just a physical meeting but also a meeting of their minds and hearts. She felt like she'd just met someone she didn't know she'd been waiting for.

She slowly collapsed on top of him, groaning at the movement.

He pulled her close. "That was so good," he whispered.

She chuckled as she stretched out fully on top of him. "It just feels so very good after the stress and the horror of the last few days."

"While we've been through hell," he said, "you have come out the other side as a strong and wonderful woman." He stared into her beautiful eyes, his fingertips grazing her face. "It'll be tough for a while, but you can survive this."

"I will," she said. "But I want to do more than survive. I want to thrive."

He looked at her and raised an eyebrow. "Are you in any

doubt over that outcome?"

She smiled and shook her head. "No, not really. I just suspect that we'll have some rough times."

"I'm not planning on ditching you," he said. "So I'll be at your side when the rough patches arrive."

She smiled and looked at him. "Really?"

"Really," he said. "I don't have to look at somebody like your sister to realize what's precious in you, and, once I found you, no way I'll let you go. So, not to worry. We're in this together." And he wrapped her up close, holding her tight.

They didn't have long because the rest of the world would intrude, but, for the moment, it was pretty hard to imagine anything interrupting this perfect moment.

She curled up in his arms and kissed him gently on the cheek. "Thank you," she whispered.

His chuckle rumbled up his chest. "No, thank you."

She flushed as she realized what he meant. "It's your turn next."

He slid a hand around her backside. "Oh, I'm not done," he said. He flipped them over, him atop her now. "I just don't know how much time we have."

Even in the distance, Gemma could hear the little girl's voice. "Apparently we don't have any time at all." She giggled, hopping off the bed and quickly redressing. She leaned over and kissed him hard. "Save it for later."

She went out to greet Tim and Becky, who were still laughing over the kittens. As she reached the front door, the little girl turned to her with a big smile on her face.

"Auntie Gemma, can we come back here next summer?" She looked up at Tim hopefully.

"Honey, you know what? We might just have to come

for a week every year. I know some of my best memories were created here."

Tim chuckled. "So the three of you would be welcome to visit us."

Epilogue

Z ACK HIGGINS WALKED into the coffee shop, took a look around, and realized neither Levi nor Ice were here yet. So he walked to the front counter and ordered himself the largest darkest coffee he could. With that in hand, he turned to look for the most isolated table and found it in the far back right corner of the coffee shop. He headed there and sat down. He tried to get here a few minutes early just because he refused to be late for meetings. He knew the last job had been only okay as far as he was concerned, having dealt with Rebecca. And the case itself had turned out all right, but the end results left him feeling very wounded in many ways.

Even now he still felt stupid, since he hadn't had a sexual relationship with Rebecca in a very long time, and the one that they had been left with for the last many years had been platonic and friendly at best. But because he'd always been hanging on to the wonderment that maybe her daughter was his, his emotional entanglements with Rebecca hadn't been severed. And that was too damned bad because he was sitting here now feeling more than a little sorry for himself, and that was as unacceptable as anything.

"There you are." Ice's warm voice broke through his musings.

He looked up and smiled. "Aren't you a picture," he

said, nodding toward her obviously pregnant belly.

"Wow, thanks, I think," she said, sitting down with a hard *thump*. "One day the baby turned, and all of a sudden I look very pregnant. And yet the baby is somehow poking all my organs. So any jokes now are *not* amusing." But her bright laugh that followed belied her words.

He smiled at the two of them, noting that Levi had come up behind him. He stood, shook Levi's hand, and asked, "Are you ready to be a father?"

"Probably not," Levi said amiably. "But, like everything, we learn as we go."

"That's a good way to look at it."

Ice looked to the coffee in front of him and asked, "Did you order anything to eat?"

"No," he said. "The traveling has been pretty rough. I'm here now though."

"Right," Levi said. "What was your analysis of the last job?"

"A shitstorm," he said instantly. "Not the job itself but for the emotional baggage that I had to get rid of."

"And have you now?" Ice asked. "With another month under your belt?"

More than curiosity was in her voice, and he wasn't exactly sure what it was. "I think so," he said with a nod. Then he grimaced and said, "I should have been. Definitely I know so. But you don't have relationships with people for years like I had with Rebecca and wonder just why you couldn't leave until this stage."

"Good," she said with that compassionate voice that he'd heard over the phone many times. "The thing is, none of us heal instantly. None of us get over anything instantly. I'm much encouraged to hear that you are realizing it's a process."

"I wish it was something that I could just hit a Delete button on the keyboard," he said. "It would make it a lot easier."

"Maybe," she said. "But the thing is, you need to be free and clear to get your head back into the game."

"As I learned all too recently," he said, staring at the mug of dark brew. "It's a little disturbing to realize just how much I did have to separate from her, when I had already thought those ties were severed." He looked over at Ice and Levi. "What's this meeting all about?"

"Just want to know where you are," Ice said. "Wondering if working for us is still something you're interested in."

"I am," he said, surprised. "I figured after the last job you wouldn't want me."

"Everybody can have a tough job," she said, "and everybody has emotional issues they have to deal with. It's all about how you deal with them that's the problem and or the solution."

"Are you sure you need more guys?" he asked, studying the two of them, hoping this wasn't some take-pity job. "You've got what? Twenty-four guys working for you?"

"Yes, but we're setting up satellite offices," she said. "One in England, one in Europe."

"Oh." He stopped and stared. "That makes sense. A jump-off point, so to speak, to get your guys' boots on the ground faster around the globe?"

"Plus networking," she said. "Our various contacts overseas have been giving us a hand setting those up."

"Well, I'm American," he said, "so I'm not sure just how that'll benefit anybody to have me on board."

"Levi is staying home for the next few months," Ice said,

"and I'm obviously grounded for at least as long."

Zack nodded. "And?" he asked, but there was further silence.

"That means we are also two men short at the compound right now," Levi explained.

"Do you have that much work?"

Ice answered, her tone firm. "Unfortunately, yes."

"Then I'm in," he said. "What can I help you with?"

"When you were in the military, ... in the navy," she said, "you worked with Bonaparte and Trent, correct?"

He chuckled. "Absolutely." Then he stopped, looked at them, and asked, "You're not thinking about hiring Bonaparte, are you?"

"Is there any reason not to?" Ice asked.

Zack thought about it, shook his head, and said, "No, I can't say that there is. They are both good men. Bonaparte just came out of a pretty ugly divorce though," he cautioned. "Not sure if he is ready to dive into something like this."

"But he didn't sign up for another tour," Levi said.

"I guess that's something you guys watch for too, isn't it?"

"Let's just say, who is staying in the navy and who's ready to come out are things we are always interested in," Ice said with a smile. "But we also need to vet the men, in particular if we don't know them."

"Got you," Zack said, smiling. "Bonaparte?" he said. "I haven't seen in a couple years, but he is a really good man, incredibly strong, but I know that the problem with his divorce was that he was *unapproachable*, as he told me."

Levi laughed at that. "I think we've all heard that one time or another."

"Well, I haven't," Zack said. "Apparently I was wearing

my heart on my sleeves anyway."

"But you're past that now," Ice said. "When you find somebody who would really be a partner in all ways, that relationship will fade into nothing, and you'll wonder what the attraction even was."

"I'm already there," he said. "At least as far as wondering what the original attraction was. I don't have any relationships, so I'm good to go, if you have something of interest."

"I have something of interest," she said, pulling out a thick file and placing it in front of her.

"What's that?"

"Possible recruits," she said. And she opened it. His picture flashed back at him. "Well, I worked on one job with Galen," he said. "I'd love to try another one."

"Trouble is, we don't do contracts," Levi said. "You are either in, or you are out."

"I think contracts might be the way to go for new recruits, a probationary period of sorts, for both sides," he said slowly, studying the lean-faced man in front of him. Levi had matured a lot over the last couple years. But then he had heavy responsibilities on his shoulders as his company took off into one of the biggest protection agencies around the world. They were known to troubleshoot and to be the guy in a tough corner, when you needed one. "You've built yourself quite a place here," he said to the two of them. They both just nodded. "It must be a little disconcerting to step back for the next few months."

"What else could we do?" she asked. "Out of necessity, we'd be keeping everybody else busy while we reduce our traveling time."

"Understood," he said. He looked as she flipped through her file. Then he saw Bonaparte's face pop out. "You know he still looks like that too," he said. "He's got a real baby face, and so everybody thinks he is this big teddy bear, but, according to his ex-wife, he just was empty emotionally."

"Any other reason for that?"

He looked at them in surprise. "His history?"

"I know his sister was murdered a long time ago," Ice said, looking up at him sharply. "Anything else?"

And Zack realized just how important all that history was when it came to hiring those men. He shook his head. "Not that I know of. I was really close to him, back in the day, but haven't seen him but a time or two now over the last couple years."

"We need a four-man team," she said. "Over in Istanbul."

"Turkey?" He stared at her in surprise. "I heard that you guys operated globally. I just hadn't realized how busy you were. As in all over the world."

"I don't know if this will stay in Turkey or not," she said, "but we've certainly covered multitudes of countries by now."

"What's the job?"

She slowly tapped the file, now closed. "The deposed president is under house arrest. As is his vice president," she said. "whose daughter has disappeared."

"By choice?"

"It's possible," Levi said, with a nod. "She is thirty-one, and she's a well-known photographer."

"I think I remember something about her," Zack said, staring off into the distance. "Zadie Nather, isn't it?"

"Yes," Levi said. "Zadie Nather. How did you hear about her?"

"She's well-known for publishing very disconcerting

photos," he admitted. "Photos about the climate change. Photos about activists. The struggle of the youths to try and regain their position in a world that they consider almost past the turning point. And I think there was something about her father being high up in the very corrupt Turkish government."

"Exactly," Ice said. "What we don't know is whether her photos have a reason behind her disappearance or whether she has disappeared herself because she didn't want to deal with the political climate in Turkey."

"I thought she was operating out of England?" Then he stopped, frowned, looked out the window, and said, "but then I remember something about Australia and the US."

"I don't think she actually has a home base," Levi said. "I think she travels around by boat."

He looked at Levi in surprise. "A houseboat?"

"A small sailing boat," he said. "How do you feel about water?"

He snorted. "I was in the navy. How do you think I feel?"

"You were a Navy SEAL, weren't you?"

He nodded. "I was," with a heavy emphasis on the "was."

"Were you caught up in that Commander Dalmatian debacle?"

He nodded. "I was. When bad orders come down, and good guys have to follow them anyway, and the good guys end up in trouble because of following the order, well, it got to be a sticky brass political scenario that I didn't like." He said, "I walked. I believe several others walked with me."

Levi nodded. "We try to keep in touch with a lot of these events," he said, "because that is where a lot of the best men come from."

"Is that how you found out about me?"

"We've had our eye on you for a while," Ice said. Then she winced, and her hand immediately went to her belly. She started to deep breathe. Levi looked over at her, an eyebrow raised. She slowly shook her head. "No, he's just arguing for lack of space."

"He?" Zack asked.

She looked at him, smiled, and said, "That's my guess."

He grinned. "I can't imagine that it would make a difference to either of you," he said warmly.

"Hell no," Levi said. "Better she has twins, and we are done with it right away."

"I'll suck at that," she said.

"Be pretty rough for the first few years though," Zack warned. "A friend of mine had twins, and all she did was change diapers for a while."

"Well, we do have friends at home just dying to get their hands on the baby," Levi said. "So Ice will have to fight to get her own diaper-changing time."

Zack grinned at that. He'd heard so much about the compound and its family environment that he couldn't imagine any child growing up there would be anything but well loved by many aunts and uncles. It was sheer magic that they managed to make it work at all. "So am I in or out?" he asked abruptly.

"You're in," Levi said. He stood. "At the bare minimum, get some zest back into your life."

"Well, put that way, how can I refuse?"

This concludes Book 22 of Heroes for Hire:
Galen's Gemma.
Read about Zack's Zest: Heroes for Hire, Book 23

Heroes for Hire: Zack's Zest (Book #23)

Zack wasn't someone to focus on his mistakes, but he'd made a big one, and it was hard to move on from it. Still he was determined to work with Levi's team to find new meaning in his life and to get his head on straight. At least that was the plan. When he ends up part of a two-man team to rescue a kidnapped woman, the daughter of a former politician, Zack doesn't know how to react—she's certainly unique. Not the least of which, she didn't appreciate the rescue. ... At least not once she learns the details.

Zadie knew her father was guilty of the crimes he'd been accused of. She was more concerned about her mother, who'd always been the downtrodden and obedient wife. But, as more and more evidence shines a light on their lives and her kidnapping, the issue is no longer as clear.

Heartbroken at the losses that keep mounting, Zadie knows she needs a second rescue—hopefully by her same rescuer. Only it's not as simple this time, and it's infinitely more dangerous ...

Find Book 23 here!

To find out more visit Dale Mayer's website.

http://smarturl.it/DMSZack

Other Military Series by Dale Mayer

SEALs of Honor

Heroes for Hire

SEALs of Steel

The K9 Files

The Mavericks

Bullards Battle

Hathaway House

Terkel's Team

Ryland's Reach: Bullard's Battle (Book #1)

Welcome to a new stand-alone but interconnected series from Dale Mayer. This is Bullard's story—and that of his team's. All raw, rough, incredibly capable men who have one goal: to find out who was behind the attack on their leader, before the attacker, or attackers, return to finish the job.

Stay tuned for more nonstop action as the men narrow down their suspects ... and find a way to let love back into their own empty lives.

His rescue from the ocean after a horrible plane explosion was his top priority, in any way, shape, or form. A small sailboat and a nurse to do the job was more than Ryland hoped for.

When Tabi somehow drags him and his buddy Garret onboard and surprisingly gets them to a naval ship close by, Ryland figures he'd used up all his luck and his friend's too. Sure enough, those who attacked the plane they were in weren't content to let him slowly die in the ocean. No. Surviving had made him a target all over again.

Tabi isn't expecting her sailing holiday to include the rescue of two badly injured men and then to end with the loss of her beloved sailboat. Her instincts save them, but now she finds it tough to let them go—even as more of Bullard's team members come to them—until it becomes apparent that not only are Bullard and his men still targets ... but she is too.

BULLARD CHECKED THAT the helicopter was loaded with their bags and that his men were ready to leave.

He walked back one more time, his gaze on Ice. She'd never looked happier, never looked more perfect. His heart ached, but he knew she remained a caring friend and always would be. He opened his arms; she ran into them, and he held her close, whispering, "The offer still stands."

She leaned back and smiled up at him. "Maybe if and when Levi's been gone for a long enough time for me to forget," she said in all seriousness.

"That's not happening. You two, now three, will live long and happy lives together," he said, smiling down at the woman knew to be the most beautiful, inside and out. She would never be his, but he always kept a little corner of his heart open and available, in case she wanted to surprise him and to slide inside.

And then he realized she'd already been a part of his heart all this time. That was a good ten to fifteen years by now. But she kept herself in the friend category, and he understood because she and Levi, partners and now parents, were perfect together.

Bullard reached out and shook Levi's hand. "It was a hell of a blast," he said. "When you guys do a big splash, you really do a *big* splash."

Ice laughed. "A few days at home sounds perfect for me now."

"It looks great," he said, his hands on his hips as he surveyed the people in the massive pool surrounded by the palm trees, all designed and decked out by Ice. Right beside all the war machines that he heartily approved of. He grinned at her. "When are you coming over to visit?" His gaze went to Levi, raising his eyebrows back at her. "You guys should come over for a week or two or three."

"It's not a bad idea," Levi said. "We could use a long holiday, just not yet."

"That sounds familiar." Bullard grinned. "Anyway, I'm off. We'll hit the airport and then pick up the plane and head home." He added, "As always, call if you need me."

Everybody raised a hand as he returned to the helicopter and his buddy who was flying him to the airport. Ice had volunteered to shuttle him there, but he hadn't wanted to take her away from her family or to prolong the goodbye. He hopped inside, waving at everybody as the helicopter lifted. Two of his men, Ryland and Garret, were in the back seats. They always traveled with him.

Bullard would pick up the rest of his men in Australia. He stared down at the compound as he flew overhead. He preferred his compound at home, but damn they'd done a nice job here.

With everybody on the ground screaming goodbye, Bullard sailed over Houston, heading toward the airport. His two men never said a word. They all knew how he felt about Ice. But not one of them would cross that line and say anything. At least not if they expected to still have jobs.

It was one thing to fall in love with another man's woman, but another thing to fall in love with a woman who was so unique, so different, and so absolutely perfect that you knew, just knew, there was no hope of finding anybody else like her. But she and Levi had been together way before Bullard had ever met her, which made it that much more heartbreaking.

Still, he'd turned and looked forward. He had a full roster of jobs himself to focus on when he got home. Part of him was tired of the life; another part of him couldn't wait to head out on the next adventure. He managed to run everything from his command centers in one or two of his locations. He'd spent a lot of time and effort at the second one and kept a full team at both locations, yet preferred to spend most of his time at the old one. It felt more like home to him, and he'd like to be there now, but still had many more days before that could happen.

The helicopter lowered to the tarmac, he stepped out, said his goodbyes and walked across to where his private plane waited. It was one of the things that he loved, being a pilot of both helicopters and airplanes, and owning both birds himself.

That again was another way he and Ice were part of the same team, of the same mind-set. He'd been looking for another woman like Ice for himself, but no such luck. Sure, lots were around for short-term relationships, but most of them couldn't handle his lifestyle or the violence of the world that he lived in. He understood that.

The ones who did had a hard edge to them that he found difficult to live with. Bullard appreciated everybody's being alert and aware, but if there wasn't some softness in the women, they seemed to turn cold all the way through.

As he boarded his small plane, Ryland and Garret following behind, Bullard called out in his loud voice, "Let's go, slow pokes. We've got a long flight ahead of us."

The men grinned, confident Bullard was teasing, as was his usual routine during their off-hours.

"Well, we're ready, not sure about you though ..." Ryland said, smirking.

"We're waiting on you this time," Garret added with a chuckle. "Good thing you're the boss."

Bullard grinned at his two right-hand men. "Isn't that the truth?" He dropped his bags at one of the guys' feet and said, "Stow all this stuff, will you? I want to get our flight path cleared and get the hell out of here."

They'd all enjoyed the break. He tried to get over once a year to visit Ice and Levi and same in reverse. But it was time to get back to business. He started up the engines, got confirmation from the tower. They were heading to Australia for this next job. He really wanted to go straight back to Africa, but it would be a while yet. They'd refuel in Honolulu.

Ryland came in and sat down in the copilot's spot, buckled in, then asked, "You ready?"

Bullard laughed. "When have you ever known me *not* to be ready?" At that, he taxied down the runway. Before long he was up in the air, at cruising level, and heading to Hawaii. "Gotta love these views from up here," Bullard said. "This place is magical."

"It is once you get up above all the smog," he said. "Why Australia again?"

"Remember how we were supposed to check out that newest compound in Australia that I've had my eye on? Besides the alpha team is coming off that ugly job in Sydney. We'll give them a day or two of R&R then head home."

"Right. We could have some equally ugly payback on that job."

Bullard shrugged. "That goes for most of our jobs. It's the life."

"And don't you have enough compounds to look after?"

"Yes I do, but that kid in me still looks to take over the world. Just remember that."

"Better you go home to Africa and look after your first two compounds," Ryland said.

"Maybe," Bullard admitted. "But it seems hard to not continue expanding."

"You need a partner," Ryland said abruptly. "That might ease the savage beast inside. Keep you home more."

"Well, the only one I like," he said, "is married to my best friend."

"I'm sorry about that," Ryland said quietly. "What a shit deal."

"No," Bullard said. "I came on the scene last. They were always meant to be together. Especially now they are a family."

"If you say so," Ryland said.

Bullard nodded. "Damn right, I say so."

And that set the tone for the next many hours. They landed in Hawaii, and while they fueled up everybody got off to stretch their legs by walking around outside a bit as this was a small private airstrip, not exactly full of hangars and tourists. Then they hopped back on board again for takeoff.

"I can fly," Ryland offered as they took off.

"We'll switch in a bit," Bullard said. "Surprisingly, I'm doing okay yet, but I'll let you take her down."

"Yeah, it's still a long flight," Ryland said studying the islands below. It was a stunning view of the area.

"I love the islands here. Sometimes I just wonder about the benefit of, you know, crashing into the sea, coming up on a deserted island, and finding the simple life again," Bullard said with a laugh.

"I hear you," Ryland said. "Every once in a while, I wonder the same."

Several hours later Ryland looked up and said abruptly, "We've made good time considering we've already passed Fiji."

Bullard yawned.

"Let's switch."

Bullard smiled, nodded, and said, "Fine. I'll hand it over to you."

Just then a funny noise came from the engine on the right side.

They looked at each other, and Ryland said, "Uh-oh. That's not good news."

Boom!

And the plane exploded.

Find Bullard's Battle (Book #1) here!

To find out more visit Dale Mayer's website.

smarturl.it/DMSRyland

Damon's Deal: Terkel's Team (Book #1)

Welcome to a brand-new series from *USA Today* best-selling author Dale Mayer, where dark-ops SEALs have special senses and skills, needed to solve intrigue, betrayal, and ... murder. A series with all the elements you've come to love, plus so much more, ... including psychics!

ICE POURED HERSELF a coffee and sat down at the compound's massive dining room table with the others. When her phone rang, she smiled at the number displayed. "Hey, Terk. How're you doing?" She put the call on Speakerphone.

"I'm okay," Terkel said, his voice distracted and tight.

"Terk?" Merk called from across the table. He got up and walked closer and sat across from Levi. "You don't sound too good, brother. What's up?"

"I'm fine," Terk said. "Or I will be. Right now, things are blown to shit."

"As in literally?" Merk asked.

"The entire group," Terk said, "they're all gone. I had a solid team of eight, and they're all gone."

"Dead?"

Several others stood to join them, gathered around Ice's phone. Levi stepped forward, his hand on Ice's shoulder. "Terk? Are they all dead?"

"No." Terk took a deep breath. "I'm not making sense. I'm sorry."

"Take it easy," Ice said, her voice calm and reassuring. "What do you mean, *they're all gone?*"

"All their abilities are gone," he said. "Something's happened to them. Somebody has deliberately removed whatever super senses they could utilize—or what we have been utilizing for the last ten years for the government." His tone was bitter. "When the US gov recently closed us down, they promised that our black ops department would never rise again, but I didn't expect them to attack us personally."

"What are you talking about?" Merk said in alarm, standing up now to stare at Ice's phone. "Are you in danger?"

"Maybe? I don't know," Terk said. "I need to find out exactly what the hell's going on."

"What can we do to help?" Ice asked.

Terk gave a broken laugh. "That's not why I'm calling. Well, it is, but it isn't."

Ice looked at Merk, who frowned, as he shook his head. Ice knew he and the others had heard Terk's stressed out tone and the completely confusing bits and pieces coming from his mouth. Ice said, "Terk, you're not making sense again. Take a breath and explain. Please. You're scaring me."

Terk took a long slow deep breath. "Tell Stone to open the gate," he said. "She's out there."

"Who's out there?" Levi asked, hopped up, looked outside, and shrugged.

"She's coming up the road now. You have to let her in."

"Who? Why?"

"*Because*," he said, "she's also harnessed with C-4."

"Jesus," Levi said, bolting to display the camera feeds to the big screen in the room. "Is it live?"

"It is, and she's been sent to you."

"Well, that's an interesting move," Ice said, her voice sharp, activating her comm to connect to Stone in the control room. "Who's after us?"

"I think it's rebels within the Iranian government. But it could be our own government. I don't know anymore," Terk snapped. "I also don't know how they got her so close to you. Or how they pinned your connection to me," he said. "I've been very careful."

"We can look after ourselves," Ice said immediately. "But who is this woman to you?"

"She's pregnant," he said, "so that adds to the intensity here."

"Understood. So who is the father? Is he connected somehow?"

There was silence on the other end.

Merk said, "Terk, talk to us."

"She's carrying my baby," Terk replied, his voice heavy.

Merk, his expression grim, looked at Ice, her face mirroring his shock. He asked, "How do you know her, Terk?"

"Brother, you don't understand," Terk said. "I've never met this woman before in my life." And, with that, the phone went dead.

Find Terkel's Team (Book #1) here!

To find out more visit Dale Mayer's website.

smarturl.it/DMSTTDamon

Author's Note

Thank you for reading Galen's Gemma: Heroes for Hire, Book 22! If you enjoyed the book, please take a moment and leave a short review.

Dear reader,

I love to hear from readers, and you can contact me at my website: www.dalemayer.com or at my Facebook author page. To be informed of new releases and special offers, sign up for my newsletter or follow me on BookBub. And if you are interested in joining Dale Mayer's Reader Group, here is the Facebook sign up page.
https://smarturl.it/DaleMayerFBGroup

Cheers,
Dale Mayer

Your THREE Free Books Are Waiting!

Grab your copy of SEALs of Honor Books 1 – 3 for free!

Meet Mason, Hawk and Dane. *Brave, badass warriors who serve their country with honor and love their women to the limits of life and death.*

DOWNLOAD your copy right now! Just tell me where to send it.

www.smarturl.it/DaleHonorFreeBundle

About the Author

Dale Mayer is a USA Today bestselling author best known for her Psychic Visions and Family Blood Ties series. Her contemporary romances are raw and full of passion and emotion (Second Chances, SKIN), her thrillers will keep you guessing (By Death series), and her romantic comedies will keep you giggling (It's a Dog's Life and Charmin Marvin Romantic Comedy series).

She honors the stories that come to her – and some of them are crazy and break all the rules and cross multiple genres!

To go with her fiction, she also writes nonfiction in many different fields with books available on resume writing, companion gardening and the US mortgage system. She has recently published her Career Essentials Series. All her books are available in print and ebook format.

Connect with Dale Mayer Online

Dale's Website – www.dalemayer.com
Facebook Personal – https://smarturl.it/DaleMayerFacebook
Instagram – https://smarturl.it/DaleMayerInstagram
BookBub – https://smarturl.it/DaleMayerBookbub
Facebook Fan Page – https://smarturl.it/DaleMayerFBFanPage
Goodreads – https://smarturl.it/DaleMayerGoodreads

Also by Dale Mayer

Published Adult Books:

Bullard's Battle

Ryland's Reach, Book 1

Cain's Cross, Book 2

Eton's Escape, Book 3

Garret's Gambit, Book 4

Kano's Keep, Book 5

Fallon's Flaw, Book 6

Quinn's Quest, Book 7

Bullard's Beauty, Book 8

Bullard's Best, Book 9

Terkel's Team

Damon's Deal, Book 1

Kate Morgan

Simon Says… Hide, Book 1

Hathaway House

Aaron, Book 1

Brock, Book 2

Cole, Book 3

Denton, Book 4

Elliot, Book 5

Finn, Book 6

Gregory, Book 7

Heath, Book 8

Iain, Book 9

Jaden, Book 10

Keith, Book 11

Lance, Book 12

Melissa, Book 13

Nash, Book 14

Owen, Book 15

Hathaway House, Books 1–3

Hathaway House, Books 4–6

Hathaway House, Books 7–9

The K9 Files

Ethan, Book 1

Pierce, Book 2

Zane, Book 3

Blaze, Book 4

Lucas, Book 5

Parker, Book 6

Carter, Book 7

Weston, Book 8

Greyson, Book 9

Rowan, Book 10

Caleb, Book 11

Kurt, Book 12

Tucker, Book 13

Harley, Book 14
The K9 Files, Books 1–2
The K9 Files, Books 3–4
The K9 Files, Books 5–6
The K9 Files, Books 7–8
The K9 Files, Books 9–10
The K9 Files, Books 11–12

Lovely Lethal Gardens

Arsenic in the Azaleas, Book 1
Bones in the Begonias, Book 2
Corpse in the Carnations, Book 3
Daggers in the Dahlias, Book 4
Evidence in the Echinacea, Book 5
Footprints in the Ferns, Book 6
Gun in the Gardenias, Book 7
Handcuffs in the Heather, Book 8
Ice Pick in the Ivy, Book 9
Jewels in the Juniper, Book 10
Killer in the Kiwis, Book 11
Lifeless in the Lilies, Book 12
Murder in the Marigolds, Book 13
Lovely Lethal Gardens, Books 1–2
Lovely Lethal Gardens, Books 3–4
Lovely Lethal Gardens, Books 5–6
Lovely Lethal Gardens, Books 7–8
Lovely Lethal Gardens, Books 9–10

Psychic Vision Series

Tuesday's Child

Hide 'n Go Seek

Maddy's Floor

Garden of Sorrow

Knock Knock...

Rare Find

Eyes to the Soul

Now You See Her

Shattered

Into the Abyss

Seeds of Malice

Eye of the Falcon

Itsy-Bitsy Spider

Unmasked

Deep Beneath

From the Ashes

Stroke of Death

Ice Maiden

Snap, Crackle...

Psychic Visions Books 1–3

Psychic Visions Books 4–6

Psychic Visions Books 7–9

By Death Series

Touched by Death

Haunted by Death

Chilled by Death

By Death Books 1–3

Broken Protocols – Romantic Comedy Series
Cat's Meow
Cat's Pajamas
Cat's Cradle
Cat's Claus
Broken Protocols 1-4

Broken and... Mending
Skin
Scars
Scales (of Justice)
Broken but... Mending 1-3

Glory
Genesis
Tori
Celeste
Glory Trilogy

Biker Blues
Morgan: Biker Blues, Volume 1
Cash: Biker Blues, Volume 2

SEALs of Honor
Mason: SEALs of Honor, Book 1
Hawk: SEALs of Honor, Book 2
Dane: SEALs of Honor, Book 3
Swede: SEALs of Honor, Book 4
Shadow: SEALs of Honor, Book 5
Cooper: SEALs of Honor, Book 6

Markus: SEALs of Honor, Book 7

Evan: SEALs of Honor, Book 8

Mason's Wish: SEALs of Honor, Book 9

Chase: SEALs of Honor, Book 10

Brett: SEALs of Honor, Book 11

Devlin: SEALs of Honor, Book 12

Easton: SEALs of Honor, Book 13

Ryder: SEALs of Honor, Book 14

Macklin: SEALs of Honor, Book 15

Corey: SEALs of Honor, Book 16

Warrick: SEALs of Honor, Book 17

Tanner: SEALs of Honor, Book 18

Jackson: SEALs of Honor, Book 19

Kanen: SEALs of Honor, Book 20

Nelson: SEALs of Honor, Book 21

Taylor: SEALs of Honor, Book 22

Colton: SEALs of Honor, Book 23

Troy: SEALs of Honor, Book 24

Axel: SEALs of Honor, Book 25

Baylor: SEALs of Honor, Book 26

Hudson: SEALs of Honor, Book 27

SEALs of Honor, Books 1–3

SEALs of Honor, Books 4–6

SEALs of Honor, Books 7–10

SEALs of Honor, Books 11–13

SEALs of Honor, Books 14–16

SEALs of Honor, Books 17–19

SEALs of Honor, Books 20–22

SEALs of Honor, Books 23–25

Heroes for Hire

Levi's Legend: Heroes for Hire, Book 1

Stone's Surrender: Heroes for Hire, Book 2

Merk's Mistake: Heroes for Hire, Book 3

Rhodes's Reward: Heroes for Hire, Book 4

Flynn's Firecracker: Heroes for Hire, Book 5

Logan's Light: Heroes for Hire, Book 6

Harrison's Heart: Heroes for Hire, Book 7

Saul's Sweetheart: Heroes for Hire, Book 8

Dakota's Delight: Heroes for Hire, Book 9

Tyson's Treasure: Heroes for Hire, Book 10

Jace's Jewel: Heroes for Hire, Book 11

Rory's Rose: Heroes for Hire, Book 12

Brandon's Bliss: Heroes for Hire, Book 13

Liam's Lily: Heroes for Hire, Book 14

North's Nikki: Heroes for Hire, Book 15

Anders's Angel: Heroes for Hire, Book 16

Reyes's Raina: Heroes for Hire, Book 17

Dezi's Diamond: Heroes for Hire, Book 18

Vince's Vixen: Heroes for Hire, Book 19

Ice's Icing: Heroes for Hire, Book 20

Johan's Joy: Heroes for Hire, Book 21

Galen's Gemma: Heroes for Hire, Book 22

Zack's Zest: Heroes for Hire, Book 23

Bonaparte's Belle: Heroes for Hire, Book 24

Heroes for Hire, Books 1–3

Heroes for Hire, Books 4–6

Heroes for Hire, Books 7–9

Heroes for Hire, Books 10–12

Heroes for Hire, Books 13–15

SEALs of Steel

Badger: SEALs of Steel, Book 1

Erick: SEALs of Steel, Book 2

Cade: SEALs of Steel, Book 3

Talon: SEALs of Steel, Book 4

Laszlo: SEALs of Steel, Book 5

Geir: SEALs of Steel, Book 6

Jager: SEALs of Steel, Book 7

The Final Reveal: SEALs of Steel, Book 8

SEALs of Steel, Books 1–4

SEALs of Steel, Books 5–8

SEALs of Steel, Books 1–8

The Mavericks

Kerrick, Book 1

Griffin, Book 2

Jax, Book 3

Beau, Book 4

Asher, Book 5

Ryker, Book 6

Miles, Book 7

Nico, Book 8

Keane, Book 9

Lennox, Book 10

Gavin, Book 11

Shane, Book 12

Diesel, Book 13
Jerricho, Book 14
The Mavericks, Books 1–2
The Mavericks, Books 3–4
The Mavericks, Books 5–6
The Mavericks, Books 7–8
The Mavericks, Books 9–10
The Mavericks, Books 11–12

Collections
Dare to Be You…
Dare to Love…
Dare to be Strong…
RomanceX3

Standalone Novellas
It's a Dog's Life
Riana's Revenge
Second Chances

Published Young Adult Books:

Family Blood Ties Series
Vampire in Denial
Vampire in Distress
Vampire in Design
Vampire in Deceit
Vampire in Defiance
Vampire in Conflict
Vampire in Chaos

Vampire in Crisis

Vampire in Control

Vampire in Charge

Family Blood Ties Set 1–3

Family Blood Ties Set 1–5

Family Blood Ties Set 4–6

Family Blood Ties Set 7–9

Sian's Solution, A Family Blood Ties Series Prequel
   Novelette

Design series

Dangerous Designs

Deadly Designs

Darkest Designs

Design Series Trilogy

Standalone

In Cassie's Corner

Gem Stone (a Gemma Stone Mystery)

Time Thieves

Published Non-Fiction Books:

Career Essentials

Career Essentials: The Résumé

Career Essentials: The Cover Letter

Career Essentials: The Interview

Career Essentials: 3 in 1

Made in United States
Orlando, FL
22 May 2022